T0064676

# VIRTUE

# VIRTUE

## LEON KING

ARCHWAY
PUBLISHING

Archway Publishing books may be ordered
through booksellers or by contacting:

Archway Publishing
1663 Liberty Drive
Bloomington, IN 47403
www.archwaypublishing.com
1 (888) 242-5904

ISBN: 978-1-4808-6892-2 (sc)
ISBN: 978-1-4808-6893-9 (e)

Library of Congress Control Number: 2018911293

Print information available on the last page.

Archway Publishing rev. date: 8/7/2020

# CHAPTER 1

**First Scene:** A gruesome crime scene in Hong Kong. Four henchmen of the Wo Che Pong crime family lie dead on the warehouse floor of a downtown clothing manufacturing plant. Their assassin is Chen Lim, son of the owners of the plant. When he refused to allow the crime lords to use his parents' business as a front to smuggle their drugs to the underboss Mr. Wang in New York City, they tried to torture him. That was their last mistake. Lim is shot during the melee and leaves the crime scene bleeding profusely. Hours later, the corrupt Hong Kong police, who are on the payroll with the Pong crime family, arrest Lim for the murders and throw him into prison. The police release a false statement to the media that the murderer was killed during an attempt by the police to apprehend him. Everyone, including his parents and family in the United State believes that Lim is dead.

**Second Scene: Summertime 2010. New York City. Mount Saint Mary High School**.

Peter Wong, Divine Ice Williams, Christian Snow, Jose Cruz, and James Robertson are sitting in science class. The boys come from wealthy families and are very popular amongst their peers. They enjoy their teacher Mr. Jackson, an ex-football player from the NFL who loves kids. The 6' 3", 250 lb. science teacher is still in good physical shape. They love his approach to teaching science because he often talks about his past experiences from the NFL and how he overcame the obstacles that he faced in his journey to the NFL along with the challenges he faced as a player.

James, who thinks he is the next Mark Zuckerberg, says to Mr. Jackson, "Man, one day I'm going to invent a way to prevent any type of computer virus by using a chip attachment."

Mr. Jackson replies, "I believe you. If you have faith and perfect your talent, anything is possible."

The kids admired the way Mr. Jackson talked with them because it seemed like he made everything he said a life-learning message. He really cared for them. The lunch bell rang at 12:00pm and the boys exited the classroom hastily to head towards the cafeteria. In the hallway, they saw Mr. Jackson, their favorite science teacher, talking to the hated school security guard Mr. Swartz, who bullied the boys and made their lives miserable every single day. It looked like he was giving Mr. Jackson a hard time. As soon as Swartz noticed the boys watching his conversation with Mr. Jackson, his demeanor quickly changed and he smiled at them. The boys were very uncertain about what kind of trouble their teacher might be in.

During lunch they all sat at the same table. At that time, they weren't the best of friends since they only really knew each other because their families reside in the same well-to-do neighborhood. They were, by far, the wealthiest kids in the school. While talking at the lunch table, they discovered that Swartz was harassing all of them. They agreed that this was strange. While the boys were discussing these strange circumstances in the cafeteria, the mean-spirited Swartz used his keys to open Christian's locker and stashed some weed to set him up. Swartz dislikes Christian's father, the powerful Miami Dolphin owner Steven Snow, who happens to own a successful number of hotel chains, resorts, and casinos, because of Mr. Snow's business ties with organized crime boss Jimmy "The Fox" Marchetti. Swartz is really an FBI agent working undercover as a security guard at the private school as part of an FBI task force running surveillance on Christian Snow and anyone connected to Mr. Snow. However, Swartz is a corrupt FBI agent who is on Jimmy "The Fox" Marchetti's payroll. Swartz is hungry for more money and power, and he is convinced he can gain both by forcing Mr. Snow to do business with him. He devises a blackmail scheme to harass Mr. Snow to the point where he will either have to work with Swartz or be turned into the FBI.

Swartz tips off to the Principal Hamlin that Christian Snow has drugs in his locker. When Swartz opens Christian's locker and the principal sees the marijuana, Christian is immediately pulled from class and sent to the detention center. When the other kids find out, they are infuriated because they know for a fact that the only kid who is familiar with drugs or any type of criminal activity for that matter is Jose Cruz, whose father is a drug dealer. He's no small timer, though. In fact, he runs the biggest drug cartel in Columbia, but he's able to maintain his image as an honest businessman due to his adept ability to launder his drug money through legitimate businesses and investments in other legitimate enterprises. When Jose and all the kids visit Christian, they realize that he's been set up. As they exit the detention center to begin heading to their next class, they observe the visibly angry Mr. Jackson speaking to Swartz in a very heated manner. They are late for their next period where the whole school will be taking the mandatory skills exam as practice for the upcoming state skills test. They hurry off. Once the exam begins, the principal releases Christian from the detention center so he may take the exam, but he promises him that he will suffer great consequences for his violation of the school's drug policy. Christian despondently walks down the hall to his classroom and passes Mr. Jackson's classroom where he hears arguing. Christian turns his head to look in the classroom and at that split second, Swartz pulls out a gun and shoots Mr. Jackson in the chest. However, there was no bang from the gunshot due to the silencer that Swartz put on his Magnum firearm. Swartz figured the hallways would be empty since the whole school would be in lockdown taking the test and had not anticipated the principal letting Christian go so early from the detention center. As Swartz turned around to make sure no one witnessed the shooting, Christian ducked and ran off silently, unseen by the murdering Swartz.

Eventually, Mr. Jackson was discovered on the floor of his classroom, bleeding with a bullet hole in his chest. He now lies in critical condition at Mercy Hospital fighting for his life with fractured ribs and punctured lungs from the bullet.

Meanwhile, Christian hurries to his girlfriend Victoria's house as soon as school lets out, shaken up and traumatized from watching the shooting of his beloved science teacher. He tells Victoria about the shooting. He tells her that he had seen Swartz earlier that day arguing feverishly with Mr. Jackson. Victoria reveals that Swartz has been hitting on her relentlessly from the first day he started at the school.

"One time he followed me after gym and cornered me in the girls' locker room while I was taking a shower. I looked up and I saw his reflection in the mirror. I screamed. He came in and locked the door. He started coming towards me, and I pleaded, "Don't hurt me. You don't have to do this. He started to take his pants off. I pushed him away as hard as I could, but he was too strong. He threw me into the shower wall, then threw me down and grabbed my breast. He overpowered me completely. Before he was about to penetrate me, I saw the girls at the door. He pulled out his gun and told me to open the door. He said, Don't say a word or I will kill you!' He hid behind the bathroom stall and when the two girls got into the showers, he ran out. I was so afraid, I feared for my life."

Christian replies, "Don't be afraid, you couldn't do anything. I'm just glad you didn't get raped or killed, but I'm going to get that dirty motherfucking cop Swartz! You just wait and see! He has gotten away with way too much dirt, and seeing Mr. Jackson get shot…I can't believe it! I need to have a private meeting with Jose, James, Divine, and Peter."

Christian sends an email to Peter, Ice, Jose, and James, revealing that the same person who shot Mr. Jackson also attempted to rape Victoria, and they needed to take action. He called a meeting at his father's vacation home on Martha's Vineyard for that coming Saturday. The boys, eager to learn the identity of the would-be killer and rapist, quickly confirm their attendance with email responses seconds after Christian's invitation.

Saturday's caravan to Martha's Vineyard was quite a sight. Jose drives an SL500 Silver Mercedes. James drives a Range Rover Truck. Divine "Ice" Williams drives a Cayenne Porsche. Peter Wong drives a red Ducati motorcycle. They arrive. Christian and Victoria have catered food ready for them from the local caterer as the meeting begins at 4pm.

Christian begins the meeting with a question. "Have you guys had any problems at the school dealing with Officer Swartz?" Everyone in the room sits up. It becomes clear to them who Christian was talking about in his email.

Christian continues. "I saw Swartz shoot Mr. Jackson in his classroom." At that point, Peter Wong, in a fit of rage, blurts out in Chinese, "That dirty bastard! I will kill him!"

Everyone in the room turns and looks at Peter. "That's not all," Victoria then reveals. "Swartz tried to rape me in the shower in the girls' locker room. If it weren't for those two girls who stayed late to take a shower, he would have gotten away with it."

The guys in the room became disgusted and incensed about how powerless and vulnerable the fine Victoria was against the powerful security guard predator who wanted to steal her innocence in the shower. Christian and Victoria swear the group to silence – that the information should remain only amongst the boys. Each member vows silence about the incidents.

Jose speaks up. "On the day we saw Swartz and Mr. Jackson arguing, I overhead Swartz on his cell phone earlier in the day telling someone "Mr. Jackson doesn't want to cooperate with us. Mr. Marchetti won't like this. That's all I heard."

Divine says, "One of my friends named Christina is a dancer at the 'X' club. She said, "Your fake security guard comes to the club all the time and meets these guys in a private room at least once a week." I know it's him because she says he has that scar on the right side of his eye. She also said that before he goes into his meetings with the men, he gives out money to the dancers like he's some kind of player or baller."

"Does your girlfriend know any of the guys he meets or the people he talks to at the club?" James asks. "Can she describe them? If so, I can do a background character profile check on my computer and get a background profile on his associates. This way, we can find out who he is doing business with and who they work for."

"That sounds good," Divine replies, "but we don't have anything on him. All that we know is that he's pissed with Mr. Jackson and that he likes to hang out at the 'X' club."

Jose nods his head. "If he has ties to any drug dealers, I can find out."

"My father has some private interest in that club," Divine says. "I will do some research to find out the day they have the meetings, who's going to the meetings, and what they're meeting about."

Victoria looks to Ice. "I want your girl's phone number. She could be in danger."

Ice replies, "You're right. I will get with her as soon as I get back to New York."

Everyone at the meeting agrees that Swartz has to be stopped. Their goal is set. The boys decide to visit Mr. Jackson. They leave Martha's Vineyard and head straight for the hospital back in New York. Mr. Jackson is still in critical condition.

# CHAPTER 2

It is Monday morning and all the kids are at school. The news hits the newspapers and all the tv cameras are waiting to interview students who know Mr. Jackson. Swartz stands in front of the school with the principal and police chief. Swartz says how Mr. Jackson was so well liked by the faculty and students.

The police chief says, "We don't have any suspects at this time, but we will do everything in our power to find the shooter."

The crowd leaves the school, and the boys go to class. Christian didn't come to school because he went to Mr. Jackson's home to do some investigating of his own. He finds the key to Mr. Jackson's home under the mat at the front door. As he's walking through Mr. Jackson's home, he enters the office den where he sees pictures of Mr. Jackson during his NFL career along with photos from his military service in the U.S. Army. He stops suddenly. He sees a picture of Mr. Jackson and Swartz in their military fatigues standing in front of a tank. Christian walks upstairs to Mr. Jackson's bedroom where he sees a picture hanging on the wall of Mr. Jackson, his father, and Swartz, all dressed in

military uniform getting off a sailboat. Then, he begins
searching through desk and dresser drawers looking for any
note or some kind of paperwork that would further link
Swartz with Mr. Jackson. In Mr. Jackson's desk drawer,
under a folder of newspaper articles, he finds a newspaper
article titled *Military Officer Shot In Ambush. Left For Dead.*
Christian continued to read.

> *Early yesterday morning, Officer Swartz
> found Corporal Jackson of C Company on
> the floor of his barracks bleeding from gun-
> shot wounds. Corporal Jackson was on duty
> guarding the Command Central Office Unit
> which houses the Army Contraband Safe. One
> million dollars was missing from the safe, and
> Corporal Jackson's key was not on him when
> he was found. Commander Snow was on call
> to the south side of the base in response to a
> bomb threat at 0800, which is the time that it
> is believed that the safe was opened. Military
> police have taken over the investigation. No
> arrests have been made.*

As he finishes reading the article, there's three loud
knocks on the front door downstairs. Christian quickly
jumps out the bedroom window, runs through the back-
yards of the neighboring houses to remain unseen by the
visitor. He finally reaches his car that he parked a few blocks
away, jumps in, and speeds off. Christian's Blackberry phone

rings. It's his dad calling from Miami on business with the football team.

"Son, are you ok?" he asks. "If you have any problem with anyone in your school, let me know. Don't hesitate to call me son."

"I'm alright. I'll let you know what is going on as I learn more."

They say good bye. Christian gets a text from Ice on his Blackberry that reads *Swartz meets with an FBI Agent named Glen Smith, a police officer name Sgt. Michael Anderson, and guess who, you're not going to believe this, one of Mr. Marchetti's personal assistants, Tony Garcia. If I get more info, I will text you back. Peace!*

In the meantime, back at the high school, Swartz is very angry. He can't find his school keys. They've been missing since the shooting on Friday. After class, Peter and James are walking in the hallway.

"I feel so bad about Mr. Jackson and Victoria," Peter says. "We can't be afraid of this guy. We've gotta find out why Swartz shot Mr. Jackson."

James stops Peter and whispers into his ear. "I did some background investigating on the internet before school this morning and found out that Swartz has been under investigation for taking bribes from various crime lords. Apparently, Swartz illegally sold some highly-classified military/combat information that he got from the FBI intelligence database to Mr. Snow through Mr. Snow's investment broker business. When the FBI found out about the transaction, Swartz said that he connected Mr. Snow to the illegal classified intelligence information while working undercover. The FBI can't find out how Mr. Snow's firm got this information without having someone on the inside with the FBI. It's clear that Swartz is trying to set Mr. Snow up for a big fall."

Suddenly Swartz approaches Peter and James from behind. "Why are you guys not in class?"

Peter looks back at him. "Why are you always riding my case, you fake cop?!"

Swartz violently grabs Peter's arm, but with mind-blowing speed and agility, he reverses the hold on his arm and now firmly holds Swartz's arm behind Swartz's back.

"Don't ever grab me again," he calmly whispers.

Swartz, struggling with Peter's arm hold, barks back, "Who do you think you are, kid? I will grab whoever I want!"

Swartz breaks free of Peter's hold and takes out his nightstick. Peter swiftly kicks it out of his hand.

Swartz says, "You think you're a tough guy, don't you?"

Then a group of students enter the hallway hugging and holding each other. Swartz storms off very upset.

Later that day in the cafeteria during lunch, James sits next to Peter. "You're a Kung-Fu expert?"

"No, my father was an orphan ninja before I came to the U.S. He taught me the way of the ninja at an early age. I teach a self-defense class at night."

"Well, after what just happened, I don't think Swartz will be harassing us anymore."

Peter shakes his head from side to side. "Yes, he will until we kill him."

The mood at the table becomes dark. They finish their lunch without saying another word.

As the school day progresses, Christian calls James on his cell phone. "Hey, man, you got some info?"

James then tells Christian about Swartz being under investigation and that his dad is somehow involved.

"I've also got some news. I went to Mr. Jackson's house and he's got pictures of himself, Swartz, and my dad when they were in the army together. There was a news article in Mr. Jackson's desk from his days in the military about him getting shot during a robbery of an army safe that he was guarding. Swartz is the one who found him."

"You could be in danger," James replied. "We've gotta do our own investigation and get to the bottom of this conspiracy!"

After Christian hangs up with James, he gets a call from Jose. "Listen, man, we need to know who is watching Mr. Jackson at the hospital because if Swartz tried to kill him, either he or someone will be back to finish the job. We need Mr. Jackson to live because Mr. Jackson knows the reason behind all this shit." Jose skips out of school early and drives past Christian's third story apartment building on Park Avenue. While driving, he calls Ice and James and tells them to meet him over at Christian's apartment. He has a plan.

So the boys meet at Christian's apartment, and the lovely Victoria answers the door dressed in silky Victoria's Secret lingerie.

"Hey guys," she says in that sweet, sexy voice.

The boys enter and sit down with Christian to talk.

Jose says, "We got a big problem. Swartz, our no good cop at school, is really an undercover FBI Agent. Everyone he is connected with are potential threats to us. If we don't

bring him and his illegal associates down, our families might
be in big trouble."

Christian was confused. "Why is it that your father was
not mentioned in the newspaper article when they were in
the army?"

Jose says, "My father has a close relationship with Mr.
Marchetti. My dad did some business with him a long time
ago. They sold guns and missiles together to small terrorist
groups in the Middle East before he funneled the funds
from his empire into legitimate businesses and investments.
Now you understand?"

"Yeah, I'm with you, man," Christian says."

James interjects. "Guys, I've gotta find out which cops
were sent to the hospital to protect Mr. Jackson." He then
pulls out his scanner chip and taps into the police scanner
and database call file. He quickly sees that detectives Cross
and Reynolds were sent to the hospital. "Oh, no," James
says. "They were sent by Swartz!"

"Where is Peter?" Jose asks?

"I was with him at school earlier today and Swartz
grabbed his arm," James replied. "Man, Peter Wong is really
Peter Lee because he reversed Swartz's grip and got Swartz
into a reverse arm hold just like Bruce Lee would. This guy
is B-A-D...BAD."

Jose pulls out his phone. "Do you have his cell phone
number?"

James says, "Yeah, I got it at lunch. Let's call him," and
gives Jose the phone to call Peter. Peter answers the phone.
"Hey, Peter, this is Jose."

"Hey, what's up?"

"I need you to go to the hospital ASAP to check on Mr. Jackson. Swartz sent some of his dirty cop friends to 'watch' him, but I don't think his boys have his best interest at heart."

"No problem," Peter says. "And if they try something with me, they won't know what hit 'em!" and he hangs up.

Ice says, "You know this problem we have to solve – it's not going to be too pretty. Are all of you ready to take responsibility to protect your family's interest?"

"What do you mean?" James asks.

"Well, the only way we can handle the problem is to kill the people associated with the problem. If Mr. Jackson lives, they'll never stop trying to kill him. Mr. Jackson's a bad ass...a stand up guy. You know he's not going to scare too easy. And you know he's not going to rat out any of our families or friends to the FBI or cops. Swartz and all the rest of the dirty cops won't stop until they get what they want." Ice looks to James. "I need information on every person associated with Mr. Marchetti and Swartz, okay? Once again, don't tell anyone. What's said in this room, stays in this room."

James nods in agreement.

Christian speaks up. "So, let me get this straight, you want us to agree on killing cops, secret agents, Mr. Marchetti, and his associates?"

Ice is stern. "Yeah, man. If we don't, lots of innocent people are gonna die!"

"Ok, what do you want me to do?"

"I need you and James to find out who else could profit from your dad being out of the picture. We need phone

2

LEON KING

records, names of business associates, and the names of
all the military personnel that your dad and Mr. Jackson
enlisted with. Also, we need all of Mr. Jackson's financial
records that you can gather. We must clear his name from
any conspiracy. Mr. Jackson is all we have. He is the only
one who knows about the situation and why Swartz tried
to kill him."

Jose chimes in. "Ok, boss, what should I do first?"

"Man," Ice says, "I'm not the boss, but I will take the
lead and try to organize our moves."

"Brother, no problem!" Jose says. "The sooner we handle
this, the better!"

Ice continues. "We need some weapons."

Jose's demeanor changes. "Wait a minute, you're talking
about a war?"

"This is War!" Ice retorts. "And I don't feel like dying in
it! This ain't gonna be no war like President Bush did where
we all became casualties of war. We're gonna win this from
the jump!"

"Ok," Jose replies. "What else do we need?"

"We need some soldiers that we can put on our payroll
to watch every move."

"No problem," Jose nods.

Ice then addresses the whole group. "We've gotta remain
undercover. No one can know we're involved."

"Let's make a toast," Christian says and raises his glass.
Everyone else follows suit. "To the family!"

As the sound of clinking glasses echoes through the
room, the bond between the boys deepens further.

"Christian," Ice says, "I need you to break into Swartz's

house and find out anything that you can. Don't forget to bring a gun and, this time, have someone with you as a lookout who will have your back." Ice's phone rings.

"We got a problem," Peter says. "Didn't you say there were two officers watching Mr. Jackson at the hospital?"

"Yeah."

"Well, I only see one outside his door."

"The other cop might be in his room."

Peter hangs up the phone and sprints down the hall to check on Mr. Jackson. The dirty cop at the door stops him.

"What do you want?"

"I want to check on Mr. Jackson."

"He's fine, but no one's to go inside. That's my order."

As Peter glances through the door, which is slightly cracked open, he sees the other cop standing over Mr. Jackson's bed with a pillow over Mr. Jackson's face. Peter hears Mr. Jackson's EKG monitor bleeping wildly and sees Mr. Jackson's arms and legs shaking violently. The dirty cop standing before Peter pulls out his sidearm and raises it to Peter's face. With catlike reflexes, Peter shakes his wrist and out comes the ninja blade secretly hidden in the cuff of his shirt. He slices the hand of the cop holding the gun, and the gun drops to the floor. As the cop winces in pain and bends over to pick up the gun, Peter darts behind the corrupt officer, breaks his neck, and sits him back down in the chair outside his room. He kicks the door to Mr. Jackson's room open and hurls a shuriken at the assassin cop who's smothering Mr. Jackson. The shuriken lands between the eyes of the cop instantly killing him and the cop falls to the floor. Mr. Jackson starts breathing again, and his EKG monitor slows down to the normal blip. Mr. Jackson is unconscious, but he's ok. Once Peter confirms that, he quickly wraps the cop's body in a sheet and stuffs it under Mr. Jackson's bed. He exits the room and puts the hat of the cop who was standing outside the door over the eyes of the corpse sitting in the chair outside Mr. Jackson's room to give the appearance of a cop taking a snooze. Peter calmly but quickly exits the hospital, jumps on his red Ducati motorcycle, and speeds off. He then calls Jose.

"It's done. The cops tried to kill Mr. Jackson, but I got to them first!"

# CHAPTER 3

**Tuesday 4am.** Swartz gets a call from the New York City Police Department. He is told to get to the hospital right away. Once he arrives, an orderly tells him that Officer Cross' body was found sitting upright in the chair outside Mr. Jackson's room. The New York City detectives onsite and Swartz enter Mr. Jackson's room where he is alive, but in critical condition, and Swartz notices a pool of blood underneath Mr. Jackson's bed. He looks under the bed and whispers.

"Oh my God. There's a dead body under the bed wrapped in a hospital sheet."

They remove the body from underneath the bed and identify the corpse of Officer Reynolds with the shuriken lodged deeply between his eyes. Swartz notices a ninja card next to the body. Some of the doctors on the crime scene briefly examine Officer Cross' body and conclude that he died from a broken neck, which is later confirmed by the autopsy conducted by the medical examiner's office.

Swartz becomes very upset and begins to cough violently. "This looks like the work of a trained assassin. We have some intelligence on these types of crimes from the past, but they've never occurred in New York." Swartz's head is swimming. He leaves the crime scene to the New York Homicide detectives and calls Agent Glen Smith immediately as he drives away. "We got a problem. The two officers I assigned to clean up the mess were killed last night at the hospital in classic ninja assassin style."

"I will look into this when I get into the office," Agent Smith says. "I might need to conduct a statewide search on all of our unsolved ninja cases."

"Call me later. I must get back home and get ready for school." Agent Smith replies, "Ok."

Swartz drives home. Susan Swartz, his wife and a successful artist whose work is on exhibit at the Philadelphia Gallery of Modern Art, greets him at the door with a kiss.

"Hey, honey. How was the art show?""It went very fine," Susan replies, "but how are you? I heard about the shooting at the school."

Swartz becomes angry. "Keep your mouth shut, damn it! I don't need my cover blown because of your big mouth!"

She tears up. "Why must you talk to me like that? I've been with you twenty years of my life. I've given you all the private space that you need and I've never questioned you about where you've been or given you a hard time about how long you've been away! This is the first time you've EVER told me to keep my mouth shut." She becomes enraged. "Is there something you want to tell me?! Is there another woman?"

"No, honey. It's nothing like that. It's just that this case has a lot of pressure on me." He apologetically says, "I don't mean to yell at you. Look, I must get going. I'll be back late, but I can't wait to see you when I get back. You look so sexy!" He gets ready for school. When he leaves, he kisses her and says goodbye.

Swartz is walking down the school hallway wondering where his keys could be because they remain missing since the shooting. The door to Mr. Jackson's classroom is still open, although the police crime scene tape still covers the door. Swartz starts looking at Mr. Jackson's desk and attempts to log on to Mr. Jackson's computer.

Principle Hamlin walks by the classroom and sees Swartz inside. "Have we found the shooter yet?"

"No, but we are doing everything in our power to find the shooter, I promise you."

The program on the flat screen tv in the hallway is interrupted by the voice of a newscaster announcing a breaking news flash: *"We interrupt this program for a News 4 Special Report. As of late last night, two New York City police officers were killed at Mercy Hospital outside the room of gunshot victim and school teacher Mr. Jackson, who remains in critical condition."* The newscast cuts to an interview with a spokesman for the NYPD who says, *"What we know right now is that Officer Reynolds and Officer Cross were killed in the line of duty last night while on security detail for Mr. Jackson. No information has been given to us as to how the officers were killed."* The news flash cuts back to the news anchor. *"More information will be provided as it is released to the media. This is a News 4 Special Report."*

Principle Hamlin relaxes. "I'm glad Mr. Jackson is still alive. Who could have done such a thing?"

At that time, the bell rings, and the students pour out of their classrooms. The crowd heads toward the cafeteria for lunch. The boys pass by the scowling Swartz outside the entrance to the cafeteria. They ignore him.

"Things are too hot right now," says Ice. "We don't need any suspensions or crap from Swartz right now."

The boys get their food and sit at the table.

Jose looks to James. "Did you get any more information?"

"Yes, Swartz is in debt to a lot of big shot people. He owes money to Mr. Marchetti. He has an arms deal that went bad. He stole 2 million dollars from the U.S. Army."

"That's good to know," Ice says.

James continues. "And he still has a real bad cocaine habit, but that still doesn't tell us why he needed to kill Mr. Jackson. Christian and I are still doing the best we can to get some answers."

Christian turns to Ice. "Have you found out when Swartz will be back at the 'X' club?"

"Yes, I got that covered. He meets on Wednesdays."

"Good," Jose says. "We must get our people in there and find out what they're planning."

"No problem," says Ice. "My girl Diamond is going to come late so that she can distract Swartz. I'm going to have her try to lure him to one of the private rooms upstairs. I'll be sure to have a bodyguard tailing her every move to keep her safe. While she is entertaining Swartz, I'll have some guys set up a video camera in the room where they have their meetings." Ice turns to Christian. "I need you to break into Swartz's house that night while Swartz is at the club to get us the information we need." Ice looks to Jose. "Jose, you make sure to get some snipers at the hospital right away. Disguise one of the snipers as an orderly and set the other sniper up in a room that is in direct view of Mr. Jackson's room so they can shoot anyone who enters the room who's not a doctor or nurse."

James frowns. "I'm sorry. I forgot to tell you that Swartz is married. She's an artist who just got back from Philly."

"That's ok," Christian replies.

"Christian," Ice says, "you've got to have back up. If she's home when you break in, that could present a problem. What kind of area does Swartz live in?"

"Long Island, in the Forest Hill Estates," James informs. "This guy lives in a mansion."

"Where is he getting the money from?" Christian asks.

"I don't know," Ice replies, "but I do know one thing – he is a criminal with a badge, and we must think like a criminal to outthink him."

"He has a big ego," Peter adds, "and men with big egos make big mistakes. Their human selfishness always gets them into trouble that their lack of control can't adjust to. Let me go with Christian. If Swartz has resistance at his house, I'd be the best one to handle it."

"Ok," Ice agrees, "but don't kill anyone unless it is life or death."

"Don't worry, Christian will be safe."

The boys leave Christian's apartment.

Peter Wong lives with his mother Linda Wong and his sister Jenny Wong in an upscale apartment building in the Soho neighborhood on Nicholas Street. Mrs. Wong is a stay-at-home mom who helps manage the family clothing manufacturing business. When Peter arrives home, Linda greets him.

"How are you doing, Peter?" She's been concerned about him because he's just not been the same since Mr. Jackson got shot.

"Ok," and he quickly heads to his room. Peter built a secret room in his bedroom that is disguised by a huge mirror. This private room contains all his ninja equipment. Peter puts on his tailor-made motorcycle suit. The bullet-proof suit contains different compartments where he carries his various knives, swords, and shuriken. Whatever situation he is dressing for, he comes prepared.

His mother knocks on the door. "Peter, I want to talk to you."

Peter opens the door.

"Peter, are you really ok? I don't want you to take this so bad, but you're acting like your brother Chen Lim did when he got killed."

"Mom, that was years ago. I am older, and this is not as bad, trust me, Mom. I'm ok. I will be right back. I'm just getting some extra class information from Christian. I missed my math class."

"Well, ok, Peter. Just be careful. I love you."

"I love you, too, Mom." Peter leaves and meets Christian at Swartz's mansion at Forest Hill Estates in Long Island. He parks his motorcycle about 4 blocks away and gets into Christian's vehicle. 2119 Forest Lane is the address. It's a large colonial duplex house sitting on about two acres of land. In Swartz's driveway is a Hummer SUV and a brand new Corvette. As they circle around to the side street Christian is amazed.

"This doesn't look like a cop's house," he says.

They find a parking spot that's inconspicuous and exit the vehicle. They sneak around to the back of the house.

"Did you see that?" Christian whispers. "It looks like a dog?"

Peter puts on his night vision goggles. "Yep, there's another dog beside a fence on the other side of the house."

"What should we do about those dogs? If we come too close to the house, the dogs will bark and wake up Mrs. Swartz."

"No problem. I'll shoot them with some toxic, non-fatal darts which will put them to sleep for about 4 hours. Then they'll wake up unharmed."

"You the man."

"I must find out if there's anyone other than Mrs. Swartz in the house." Peter scans the inside of the house through the windows with his night vision goggles, which also serve as high-powered binoculars. He sees another dog inside the house. He tells Christian, "I see Mrs. Swartz in her room. For us to get inside we must enter through the patio doors. I don't see a lock on them, which should make an easy entrance for us."

"What are we going to do about Mrs. Swartz?"

"I have toxic, non-fatal darts for humans as well. Ok, Christian, this is the plan, and we must move fast. You're going to stay outside and keep your eyes on the front of the house. Keep your phone on vibrate. I've done this same thing before. I'm going to cut the alarm off and sneak into the backyard. I'll lure the dog with some food and when he comes to the door, I'll hit him with the dart. I'll enter the house, find Mrs. Swartz, and hit her with the dart as well."

"Ok, no problem, Peter. Just be careful."

Peter sneaks into the backyard, disconnects the wires of the alarm system at the panel, and silently scurries up the patio to the back doors. He quietly opens the door and enters, but lying on the floor is a dog that Peter didn't see on his initial scan of the house. The dog wakes up and barks one time. Peter quickly throws the dart, which puts the pooch immediately to sleep. The other dog, who heard the single bark of his companion, comes running around the corner, and Peter stealthily shoots the second dog with the dart and puts the dog down with speed.

Upstairs, Mrs. Swartz thinks that she hears something. She walks down the stairs and calls to her pets. "Bruno! Aston! Here, baby!" but she receives no answer. As she enters the kitchen and looks down at the floor, Peter sneaks up behind her and throws a dart in her neck. She immediately passes out, and Peter catches her before her limp body can hit the kitchen floor. He gently lies her down.

Peter enters the room next to the kitchen and sees family pictures on the library cabinet. Then he proceeds upstairs. He looks in several rooms until he finds an office where Swartz keeps a safe and a large file cabinet. He opens the drawers and finds several documents that reveal his secret military arms deals. He also finds several folders containing surveillance photos - one folder that contains photos of all the crime lords in New York. Another folder contains photos of all the boys at different locations. He finds photos of Christian and his dad in Miami on a boat. Peter begins looking through another file folder and finds pictures of Mrs. Swartz in a restaurant with another man. He is young with dark hair.

He finds another picture of Mrs. Swartz going into a hotel with the same man. He calls Christian on his cell phone and tells him what he found. Then he wires Swartz's office with microphones and installs a hidden surveillance camera. He also puts a wire in Swartz's uniform. He leaves the office and enters the master bedroom where he sees mail and other documents on the side desk by the bed. He sees airline tickets for a flight to Boulder, Colorado, in two weeks. Before Peter leaves the house, he realizes he should probably check the garage. There he finds Swartz's CLS Mercedes truck. Inside the vehicle, he sees a golf club with a *Hyatt Hotel Resort Golf Club Max* sticker on it. Then Peter leaves the garage and exits the house through the back patio doors. He rewires the alarm system at the panel to turn the alarm back on and meets Christian around the back of the house.

Peter says, "Christian, let's go to the Big Wong Restaurant in Chinatown for dinner?"

While the boys eat and discuss Peter's discoveries, Peter's cell phone rings. It's his mother. She's upset.

"I got a call from the hospital about your sister Jenny. The cancer is spreading, and the doctors don't expect her to live much longer."

Peter is very troubled by this news. Jenny and Peter grew very close after the death of their brother years ago. Peter immediately gets up from the table and says, "I must go see my sister."

"I understand."

They depart.

Meanwhile, Ice calls Christian. "How did you and Peter do with the Swartz house?"

"Other than a few attack dogs, we did fine."

"Did you guys hurt anyone?"

"No, your man Peter took good care of them."

"Where is Peter now?"

"He had to go to the hospital. His sister is dying from terminal cancer."

"I'm so sorry to hear that. Keep me updated."

"I will."

"I gotta go. Swartz's associates are getting ready to meet in the club."

In the meantime, Swartz is being entertained by Diamond in the private Desire Suite at the 'X' club. Ice's bodyguard is keeping a close eye on the suite to ensure the dancer's safety. All of a sudden, the bodyguard's cell phone starts buzzing. He's got a new text message from Swartz. *There's a fight downstairs, someone needs to go handle it.* The bodyguard leaves the suite area to take care of the fight downstairs, and he calls Ice on his cell phone.

"There is no fight!" Ice screams. "Get back to that damn room right now, you stupid fool!"

In the Desire Suite, Swartz puts a gun to Diamond's head and warns her to not say a word. The terrified dancer complies. He locks the door to the front of the suite and takes her out the back door of the club. The bodyguard runs back to suite, but the door is locked. He calls Ice back.

"The door of the Desire Suite is locked and I don't think Swartz and the young girl are in there."

"Break down the damn door!"

He and two other bodyguards on Ice's payroll break

down the door, and he's right, Swartz and the dancer are gone.

Meanwhile, out back, Swartz says to Diamond, "Now I got you just where I want you."

"You punk cop!" Diamond barks. "My boyfriend will kill you if anything happens to me!"

"Shut up, bitch!" and with those words he smacks her down to the ground. He jumps on her and puts one of his hands over her mouth. He begins to rip off her dress.

The struggling Diamond somehow finds an empty beer bottle on the ground and smashes it on Swartz's head. She pierces the night with loud screams.

The bodyguards hear the screams and make their way to the back of the club where they find Swartz wrestling with Diamond. They pull Swartz off Diamond and subdue him.

Swartz yells out, "Do you know who I am, you stupid nigger?!"

The head bodyguard gets in Swartz's face. "I got your nigger right here," and shows his gun. "You goin' to re-member who this big black nigger is if you don't take your motherfucking ass out of here!"

Swartz then shows his gun. By that time, every body-guard in the club is out back. Divine stays inside to remain anonymous. Divine calls the head bodyguard on the phone.

The bodyguard asks Ice, "What do you want us to do with Swartz? He was back here trying to rape your girl!"

Get that sorry white sucker off this property. Don't hurt him. I will take care of him at another time!"

Swartz is escorted by the team of bodyguards off the property with a few kicks and punches.

In the meantime, Swartz's associates were meeting in the private room as usual, but they heard about the melee in the back of the club. They decided to cut the meeting short and reschedule for another time.

Mr. Marchetti says to the group, "This guy Swartz is really a problem, but he owes us too much money to get rid of him yet. So, for now, let us wait. But when he comes up with the 20 million he owes us, he's a dead man!"

FBI Agent Glen Smith, a member of the meeting, excuses himself to go to the bathroom. He calls Swartz on the phone. "Hey, man, what is wrong with you?! Why are you trying to rape a dancer?! You could ruin the day for a piece of ass!"

"You don't know what you're talking about! That bitch is the girlfriend of Divine Ice Williams, and I know she's recognized me and ratted me out to Ice. His father owns 60% of the 'X' club, remember? If I can get to Ice's father, I can make him pay me to get the heat off of him!"

"But being a partner in a strip club doesn't make him a criminal! What crime has he committed?"

Swartz replies, "All I have to do is plant a lot of drugs in his home, get a judge to sign off on a search warrant, and arrest him! He would have to bend. We bribe him for at least 20 million for the money we owe to the group."

"But how do you know he can get it?"

"Are you crazy?! This guy they call Polo Man makes at least 20 million a year in concerts alone. The club makes 15 million a year and his net worth is at least 260 million dollars. You know I do my research."

Agent Smith replies, "So, this is why you've been visiting

club 'X' and made it the regular place for the meetings of the group!"

Swartz replies, "Yes, it's all a plan to extort money from him and his empire."

Agent Smith says, "Man, be careful, if you don't come up with the money, they're going to kill you."

Swartz pulls up and parks his car in the driveway outside of his house and snorts a few lines of cocaine. He is an addict, and he is wired up to the racks. Sweating and out of control, pressed to find a way out of debt.

Swartz enters his house about 6am on Thursday morning, and he notices something strange. The dogs haven't come running to greet him. It dawns upon him that he didn't hear the dogs barking when he pulled up into the driveway. He enters the kitchen, turns on the light, and finds Susan lying on the floor. He's panicked. She is just waking up and seems very groggy and confused. She tells Swartz that she heard Bruno, their Rottweiler, bark once the night before. Swartz hurries to the other side of kitchen where he finds the dogs Bruno asleep on one side and Aston on the other. He tells his wife to stay there. He looks at Bruno's neck, the dart is still there. He sees another dart laying next to Aston.

"Susan, wait here. I'm going to check the rest of the house." After he nervously makes sure no intruders are still present, he immediately calls Agent Smith and explains that he found his wife and two dogs inside passed out on the floor from what appears to be some kind of tranquilizer darts. "My wife is conscious, but the dogs are still out," says Swartz.

Agent Smith asks, "Are you going to call the police?"

"Yes. I don't know who this is, but the same type of dart was found at the crime scene at the hospital. My wife could have been killed or this could have been an attempt to kill me." Swartz calls the New York City PD and they come to the house. When they arrive, the dogs are still asleep.

Mrs. Swartz, shaking and trembling screams, "What is going on, David?! Someone tried to kill us!"

Swartz tries to comfort her. "I'm sorry, honey. Trust me. I will find out who did this, I promise you."

The detectives search inside and outside and they find two other dogs asleep in the back yard.

Susan asks Swartz, "What happened to your head? You have a deep cut on it."

"I slipped on the floor of the bathroom of the club we're detailing."

As the detectives search through the house they discover a ninja drawing card in the kitchen by the back patio door.

The lead detective pulls Swartz aside. "Man, this does not look too good. It seems to me to be either some kind of warning to you or they were trying to kill your wife and got scared off. Maybe you and your wife should get out of the house and relax for the day."

Swartz replies, "Thanks, but we will be alright."

Meanwhile, Ice brings Diamond back to his gigantic colonial home in Jamaica, Queens, on 158 and Hollis Avenue.

"Are you ok, Diamond?"

"My lip hurts."

"I am so sorry, sweetie. I would have killed that motherfucker myself, but we must figure out why he tried to kill

Mr. Jackson. But after we find out why, he's a dead cop." He gently kisses her, and they begin to make love in the living room. They're interrupted by the cell phone. It's James.

"Hey, Ice. What's up?"

"I'm good, but can you call back. I'm kinda busy."

"Ok, but there's some real shit going down with Swartz and his associates. I just got the tape from tonight at the club, and Swartz is in a lot of trouble. He owes 20 million, and if he doesn't get the money, they're gonna kill him."

"WHAT?!"

"Yeah! And the FBI Agent Glen Smith is scared. He skipped out of the meeting, and one of the bodyguards spotted him on the phone in the bathroom talking with Swartz."

"Well, James, thank you, man. I will see you in school. We all had a long night. Let's try and get some sleep so we can get to school on time." Ice lies back down with Diamond, and they resume their love making.

James calls Jose, who is at home counting money and cleaning some guns. (He's an excellent shooter.) Jose's been in close contact with the hospital sniper team that is under-cover watching Mr. Jackson.

"What's up?"

James says, "Listen, man, we've got a big problem with Swartz. He owes 20 million dollars to his associates, and Mr. Marchetti's one of them. You told me how big he is because of the relationship your father has with him. These men are putting a lot of pressure on Swartz, which is going to cause him to take some drastic measures to pay off this huge amount of money. This guy is very dangerous."

Jose replies, "I think Mr. Jackson knew about some money or he won't give him the information on someone. Whatever he has on Swartz, it is enough information to get him exposed or killed. We must keep Mr. Jackson alive. Let's talk at school about this with the boys tomorrow."

Peter calls Christian from his home.

"What's up?" Christian asks.

Peter says, "Hey, I wanted to ask you something. Didn't you say your dad owns a ski resort in Colorado?"

"Yes, why?"

"I found plane tickets for a flight to Colorado for the end of the month."

Christian says, "We've got to find out what business he's doing in Colorado and whether my father is planning to be in Colorado at the same time."

"This guy is definitely meeting your dad. We must find out what the meeting is about or does your dad even know that Swartz will be in Colorado. Have you talked to Jose or James?"

Christian says, "No, I haven't. I did speak with Ice, but he didn't tell me what happened at the club 'X' meeting yet. We'll see him tomorrow at school and we can find out what happened at club 'X'."

The next day in school, the boys meet for lunch in the cafeteria.

Ice says to the group, "Guys, we had a very busy night last night."

In unison, everyone responds, "Yeah, you got that right!"

Jose remarks, "This is just the beginning. We are just getting started."

Principal Hamlin comes over to the boys' table. All the guys greet Mr. Hamlin.

Principal Hamlin asks the group, "Did you hear the news about Officer Swartz?"

Ice replies, "No, what happened?"

"Mr. Swartz called in this morning to notify me that he wouldn't be at work today because his house was broken into last night, and the NYPD were at his house conducting an investigation."

Christian insincerely says, "I'm sorry to hear that" with a feigned expression of concern on his face.

Principle Hamlin replies, "Boys, I hope you are staying out of trouble, we don't need anymore negative exposure to this school."

The group reassures the principal, "No, Mr. Hamlin, we got your back. If we hear anything, we will let you know."

Principal Hamlin replies, "Ok, boys, thanks and have a great day!"

Meanwhile, Mr. Marchetti tells his assistant Tony Garcia to call Swartz to schedule a lunch meeting with Mr. Marchetti. The Fox doesn't like to be stood up. He didn't appreciate Swartz missing the regular meeting of the associates at the club.

Tony Garcia calls Swartz. "Hello, this is Tony. How are you doing?"

Swartz replies, "Well, things could be better. My house was broken into last night. Times are hard and people are under pressure. For some, the only way to survive is to steal or they starve."

Tony replies, "Yeah. Look, Mr. Marchetti wants to

see you for lunch at 1pm at the Rockefeller Hotel Olives restaurant."

Swartz says, "But I'm finishing the investigation at my house."

Tony replies, "This is not a formal invitation that you can RSVP for. This is a request from Mr. Marchetti for your presence or else! Your investigation will continue, we won't stop it."

Swartz responds, "Thank you, no problem."

Tony says, "Good," and hangs up.

Swartz prepares for his lunch meeting with The Fox, but Susan is still very upset about last night.

"I thought you would stay home today and have lunch with me," Susan pleads.

Swartz replies, "I wish I could, honey, but crime never leaves this city, and I must check out some intel that we got on Mr. Jackson's shooter."

Susan says, "Ok, but, please come back early because I'm afraid."

Swartz responds, "Don't worry, I have police on standby watching the house to protect you."

Meanwhile, the boys are still eating lunch in the cafeteria. Ice tells everyone what went down at the club, and Christian tells everyone what Peter found at Swartz's house.

James says, "I just got from Swartz's house that he's going to meet with Mr. Marchetti at 1pm at the Rockefeller Hotel Olive Restaurant."

Ice then says, "Let me make a phone call. I think I can get someone I know to drop past that restaurant with his girl and eavesdrop on that meeting."

Jose says, "Cool. Do you need anything?"

Ice replies, "Yeah, man, I might need a piece. Can you hook my friend up?"

Jose says, "Sure, no problem, what's his name?"

Ice says, "His name is Rico. He owns a meatpacking business in midtown."

Jose replies, "No problem. Consider it done. I will get one of my boys to leave him a package at his meatpacking company by noon. Just text me the name and address so I can make this happen."

James says to the group, "Guys, we need to get ready for Swartz's next move. Believe me, he won't be happy with his meeting today, and the heat is going to push him right into our hands. But with his FBI friend Agent Smith, we can't be too sure what his next move will be."

# CHAPTER 4

Meanwhile, Diamond decides to visit Victoria at her East Manhattan condo by 69th Street. Diamond calls Victoria.

"Hey, girl."

Victoria replies, "What's up, Diamond?"

"I've decided to come over. I'm still shook up about last night, and I just want to talk to a friend."

"Okay," says Victoria. "That's fine. I'll be waiting for you. Wow, I'm sorry, here's my address so you can GPS it – 1638 East 69th Street. I'm on the lower east side by the river."

"Ok, I will be there shortly." Diamond then calls Ice. "Hey, sweetie."

Ice replies, "Hey, what's up?"

"I'm going over Victoria's house."

Concerned, Ice says, "Do you feel alright to do that?"

Diamond replies, "Yes, I want some company. I want to talk to Victoria. She's real sweet."

"Ok, just be careful." Ice thinks for a second. "Let me get my boy Skip to drive you."

Diamond replies, "C'mon, sweetie. I'm going to be fine." She hangs up and gets in the car to drive to Victoria's.

After Diamond hung up, Ice called his boy Skip and

told him to follow her anyway. It wasn't worth getting into an argument with Diamond about it. Ice felt better knowing that his boy Skip had his girl's back. He told Skip on the phone, "Call me if any problems come up." It was the right thing to do, he thought to himself. Ice tells Christian, "Our girls are getting close, and we've got to protect them."

Christian agreed. Unfortunately, no one was aware that Swartz was having surveillance conducted on Diamond by the FBI. As she's driving to Victoria's house, she's being tailed by an unmarked car.

After being on the road for about 30 minutes, Diamond calls Ice and says, "Hey, sweetie, do you have anybody that works for you that drives a light blue Impala?"

Ice replies, "No, I don't."

Peter overhears Ice's conversation with Diamond and says, "I've got to run to the hospital to check on my sister."

Ice tells Diamond, "Stay calm and keep driving to Victoria's house. I've got someone on the way to follow you."

Diamond asks, "You called Skip and told him to follow me anyway, Ice?"

"Yeah, I told you I'm not letting anything happen to my sweetie." Ice hangs up with Diamond and calls Skip who is supposed to be trailing Diamond for her protection. "Man, where are you at? My girl called and she's being followed."

Skip replies, "I couldn't get my car started, and that's what held me up."

Ice barks, "Man, you got to push it! My girl is in trouble! The cops are trailing her, and I don't know what they might pull."

Skip replies, "I gotcha, bro!" and hangs up.

Meanwhile, Peter wasn't really going to the hospital. He was speeding on his motorcycle to catch up with Diamond to make sure she safely arrives at Victoria's. Diamond is driving Ice's Porsche Cayenne. (He's also got a Black Range Rover Sport).

At this point, Christian calls Victoria back. "I heard about Diamond coming over. She's being trailed by the police. You might want to keep her calm."

Victoria replies, "Ok, I'll call her." They hang up, and Victoria attempts to call Diamond, but there's no answer. Victoria's car is being side-swiped off the road by the cop in the light blue Impala. Ice's boy Skip is nowhere to be found. Meanwhile, Peter is speeding to Victoria, he gets on the 9th street tunnel and he's about 2 miles away from the east side. He finally sees Ice's Porsche on the side of the road. An undercover cop in a suit is talking to Victoria through the open window of the Porsche. She's sitting in the car. Peter stops his bike about 30 yards away to sneak up on the cop.

The cop suddenly pulls out his gun, points it at Diamond, and screams, "You little bitch, get out of the car!"

Peter walked up to the Porsche and says to the cop, "Is there a problem, sir?"

The dirty cop turns, says, "No," and begins to fire shots at Peter. But Peter's able to avoid the flying bullets by dropping down to the ground on the other side of the Porsche with lightning-quick speed. The cop drops to the ground to shoot Peter under the car. Peter leaps over the Porsche and pulls out his samurai sword. The cop lifts up his head and fires off one more shot. Peter avoids the bullet and swiftly decapitates the dirty cop.

Diamond exits the vehicle and runs into the street screaming, "Help! Help! Help!"

Peter throws two ninja cards on top of the car and speeds off on his red Ducati motorcycle.

Ice's friend Skip finally arrives at the scene and screams at Diamond, "Get in the car! Let's go!"

Meanwhile, the meeting has started at the Rockefeller restaurant between Swartz and Mr. Marchetti. Swartz is extremely nervous and scared.

Mr. Marchetti begins, "How are you, David?"

Swartz replies, "I'm ok."

Mr. Marchetti answers, "That's not really honest, now, is it, David, based on the circumstances that have transpired since last night? Actually, it looks like you're in a lot of horse-shit, don't you think, David?

Puffs of smoke from his oversized Cuban cigar waft into the air and The Fox drinks more red wine. The Fox is about 6' 2" and weighs about 300 lbs. Mr. Marchetti continues, "David, how is your wife doing with her art?"

Swartz replies, "She's doing fine."

Mr. Marchetti says, "I would like to see some of her work some time."

"Sure," replies Swartz. Swartz's cell phone rings. It's Agent Smith. He tells Swartz that the undercover agent that Swartz had following Diamond was decapitated on the 9th Street Parkway earlier by someone with a samurai sword. Swartz cups his hand over the phone and asks Mr. Marchetti, "Can I take this call real quick?"

Mr. Marchetti says, "No problem. Don't be too long. I don't want my alfredo pasta to get cold."

Swartz gets up from the table and walks out the front door and says, "Ok, I'm back."

Agent Smith says, "What should we do?"

Swartz replies, "We must find that bitch. She'll know who killed our FBI Agent Rick Waters who's been on the force for 25 years. This ninja shit is going to be a problem if we don't find the killer ASAP. Have you got any intel?"

"The ninja cards are from ancient China, the 1800s it looks like, but that's all we have right now. I'm waiting for more info from the Hong Kong police detective files."

Swartz says, "Ok, I've gotta get back to the meeting with The Fox."

Smith replies, "Be careful, man."

Swartz sits back down at the table.

Mr. Marchetti says, "Anything wrong, David?"

"No, just crime in the streets of New York City, that's all."

Mr. Marchetti says, "It seems like you got a problem, David. This cop killer is causing some of my close business associates to be very nervous and reluctant about doing business with us until this killer is stopped. We don't need any extra exposure from some undercover assailant killing our soldiers. You don't even know who he is or what he wants. David, you owe us A LOT of money. I need you to get this murdering bastard off the streets! I don't want any of my partners falling victim to this lunatic assassin. We need you to fix this problem or ELSE! Now, back to my money. Do you have any idea as to when we can settle our account?"

Sweating and fidgety, Swartz nervously replies, "I'm working on it, Mr. Marchetti."

The Fox responds, "And I'm working on killing you

if I don't get an answer by the end of this month." Mr. Marchetti laughs loudly. "Now eat your pasta, David, it's getting cold. Please forgive me for my poor hospitality." He turns to the waiter, "Waiter! Bring more wine." He looks to Tony, "Tony, get me another cigar from my briefcase."

At school, Ice's cell phone rings. It's Diamond. She wants him to come to Victoria's house. Ice leaves school for Victoria's with Christian and Jose following. Once everyone arrives at Victoria's, they begin discussing what happened.

Jose asks Diamond, "Who was the man on the motorcycle that killed the cop with the sword?"

Diamond replies, "It all happened so fast. I think it was Peter, but he didn't stay, the guy sped off as quickly as he saved me."

Ice says, "Are you sure?"

Diamond responds, "Yeah, I can tell by the motorcycle."

The doorbell rings. It's NYPD. They ask for Diamond.

The first cop says, "We need to talk to you. We need you to come down to the 61st precinct."

Ice asks, "We can't talk right here?"

The officer barks back, "Who asked YOU? You got a problem? Because I ought to run your black ass down there also!"

Ice replies, "No problem, officer, anything for the NYPD."

They take her down for questioning. The boys decide to send Jose with her to the police station.

Ice says, "Christian, stay here with your girl."

Christian replies, "Ice, what are you going to do?"

Ice responds, "I'm going to the club. I've got to get in touch with Peter so we can talk."

They all split up. All this time, Peter has been hiding behind the building watching Victoria's house. He follows the cops, who have Diamond in their squad car, to the police station. Diamond notices Peter in the side mirror about 12 car lengths behind the squad car. She feels safe. They arrive at the precinct, take her to a private interview room, and begin their interrogation regarding the death of the undercover FBI agent.

The first detective asks Diamond, "Did you see the killer?"

She responds, "I don't have to answer any questions without my lawyer being present."

The detective says, "Do you want us to keep you here until you call your lawyer? Just answer my damn question!"

Diamond begins to cry. Meanwhile, Peter scales the police station wall with his hand claws. He enters the police station through a window and begins sneaking down the back hallway. He hears the footsteps of two police officers walking towards him. He suddenly throws his ninja grappling hook at the ceiling and hoists himself upside down at the top of the wall. The cops walk past unaware of his presence. As he hears the footsteps fade away, he jumps down off the wall and resumes heading down the hallway. Peter's cell phone buzzes. It's Ice.

Ice screams, "Didn't I tell you NOT to kill anyone!"

Peter calmly responds, "It's too late for that."

Ice barks back, "Why did you kill the cop on the 9th Street Parkway?!"

Peter whispers, "Well, if I didn't kill him, you wouldn't have a girlfriend."

Ice asks, "The cops tried to kill her?"

Peter says, "What do you think? I lost a brother because of dirty cops. You guys are all I have. My sister is dying of cancer. I refuse to let the cops just take away all the people I care for on this earth."

Ice asks, "What happened to your brother?"

Peter replies, "My brother killed four cops who tried to kill my father because they were dirty Hong Kong cops who were trying to destroy my father's business. They shot and killed my brother, and took my father away when I was 12-years old. All I heard was that he got shot in the street leaving the crime scene."

Ice replies, "I understand. Where are you, Peter?"

Peter responds, "I'm at the 61$^{st}$ precinct protecting your girl."

Ice says, "Be careful."

As soon as Peter hangs up with Ice, the two cops who were previously walking down the hall spot Peter. They draw their weapons. Peter hurls a non-fatal sleeping dart at one of the officers and hits him. He falls to the ground immediately. The other officer fires off a shot that misses Peter and hits the wall behind him. Suddenly, two additional officers begin running towards Peter. He hurls a smoke bomb that stops them in their tracks because the smoke burns their eyes and makes it impossible to see anything. Peter disappears. The police station is on alert with cops running around searching for Peter. The cops interrogating Diamond join the search for "The Sniper" (his nickname that the police are now calling him). The door opens to Diamond's interrogation room. It's Peter.

The stunned Diamond says, "How did you get in here, Peter?!"

Peter laughs and says, "I walked in like you!"

Diamond replies, "You're funny! I'm ok, but if they catch you, we're both in trouble!"

Peter responds, "Don't worry, I got your back!"

Diamond says, "I believe you!"

He exits the room, and two more cops appear. He throws two shurikens, which kills the two officers, and he leaps out of a nearby window. He jumps on his Ducati motorcycle and leaves the scene without a scratch. When the cops realize that "The Sniper" infiltrated their police station and killed their fellow officers, they become furious with anger. The head of the 61$^{st}$ precinct, Commissioner Robert Cole, calls Swartz. Swartz arrives at the police station, and the detective briefs Swartz about the killing on the 9$^{th}$ Street Parkway and about the fiasco at the police station as well.

He says to Swartz, "These situations seem to be related. We must find the connections between the 9$^{th}$ Street killing, the killing at the hospital, and what happened here tonight."

Swartz responds, "This is a conspiracy against New York City cops, that's all. We need to find someone who has a personal vendetta against NYC Cops. This person has probably been arrested, had done time, and has an issue with whoever caught him. We should start there."

Commissioner Cole says, "That makes sense. Let's focus on this case a bit deeper. I need more information on any cop who arrested and convicted a sniper or some ninja or whatever in the past."

Swartz replies, "Let me talk to the girl you brought here." Swartz enters Diamond's interrogation room. Swartz says, "Remember me?"

Diamond replies, "How could I forget your ugly face? I hope you don't think I'm talking to you, you fucking creep! I hope my boyfriend kills you!"

Swartz growls back, "You better hope you even see your boyfriend again, you little bitch!" He calms down and quietly asks her, "Do you know the person who killed the cop?"

Diamond replies, "I don't know him, but I wish I did, I feel just like him. You cops are no good and you think you're going to get away with this!"

Swartz says, "You're in a bad position to be talking smack about the position we're in as cops. You're the one that appears to me to be an accessory to a crime." He draws closer to Diamond, "And if I don't get some answers, you might be keeping us company here."

# CHAPTER 5

SCENE: A maximum security prison in Hong Kong. Prisoner Chow Lim Wong. Chow Lim's plan to escape is in action. Lim swallows the Rohypnol pill that he stole from the hospital prison. He knows that it will knock you out temporarily. The hospitals use it to knock out irate prisoners to transport them back to their cells. The guards notice that he is not present for roll call and see that he is unresponsive on his bed. He is taken from his cell to the prison hospital ER room. As they transport him to the ER, Chow Lim manages to steal the keys from one of the guards while he's not paying attention. In the ER room, all but one doctor exits the room. The lone ER doctor is leaning over Chow Lim checking his heart rate with his stethoscope. Chow Lim's eyes open suddenly and he bites the lone doctor by his teeth breaking his nose. The doctor falls to the floor unconscious. Chow Lim falls out of the bed still restrained with handcuffs on his wrists and shackles on his feet. He used the guard's keys to open his handcuffs and leg irons. He removed the doctor's uniform and put it on. He stole some syringes and walked out into the hallway where he spots the first guard. He sneaks up behind him and chokes him. As the guard fell to the ground, Mr. Lim removed his firearm and keys. As he runs through the prison and manages to get to the exit, all the prisoners are shouting and screaming. Prison guards are scrambling all over the yard and the guards in the towers begin shooting at him. He's able to dodge the bullets and he shoots the two guards in the sniper positions on the far towers. Two more correctional officers appear and attempt to corner him, but he leaps over an 8-foot barrier wall and uses it as a shield from the additional snipers and other correctional officers. He shoots two more officers who dart around the corner of the wall. As he makes his way closer to the gate, the guards release the attack dogs. However, he has at least a 60 yard distance between them, so he's able to climb and claw his way up the barbed wire gate. A bullet hits his leg. But with his adrenaline pumping and freedom in sight, he ignores the pain and he leaps over the top of the barbed-wire fence to the other side. As he lands, the attack dogs are barking wildly and trying to climb the fence to pursue him. He plunges into the lake outside of the prison and swims feverishly to the other side. He hears helicopters and then the sounds of boat motors and more barking dogs. The Chinese police are hot on his tail. Mr. Lim has been planning this escape for some time. His accomplice Tina Zinn was a cook who worked in the prison. She's his only friend on the outside who he's kept secret until this day. She picks him up in her vehicle, and they travel the backroads until they reach the closest city to Hong Kong. Lim is in love with Tina Zinn, but she's aware of his plan to travel to New York to visit his brother. For now, he's elated to be with her.

Meanwhile, Mr. Jackson has been in Mercy hospital for

two weeks now. He's beginning to recover, but he's really not cognizant of where he is. In his mind, he can still see Swartz's face right before Swartz shot him. Mr. Jackson sweats from the trauma of the shooting. Mr. Jackson, who is now alone, has a daughter named Tonya that lives in Washington, D.C., and works as an executive assistant to DC Mayor Vincent Gray.

Tonya receives a phone call from the hospital, "Hello, Ms. Jackson, this is Dr. Neil Anderson. I'm the senior surgeon at Mercy Hospital. I just wanted to give you an update on your dad's progress. He is fully awake now from the trauma to his lungs and his rib fracture. He has a good chance of a full recovery in a few months."

Tonya replies, "Thank God. I've been praying so much. Thank you so much, Dr. Anderson. You really blessed my day."

Dr. Anderson replies, "No problem. When are you coming back to New York?"

She replies, "I had planned to come this weekend."

Dr. Anderson says, "Good. I will see you this weekend then."

Officer Jim Callahan overhears the conversation regarding Mr. Jackson's progress and calls Swartz. "Hello, sir. I've got news here at the hospital that Mr. Jackson is able to speak, but very slowly, and he's able to open his eyes."

Swartz says, "Thanks, Officer Callahan." Swartz immediately calls Agent Smith and tells him the good news. Swartz says, "I need to talk to him without any interruptions from any doctors or family members like his daughter Tonya."

"Ok, but we've got to move fast because if he tells the NYPD you tried to kill him, we're done."

Swartz agrees, "I've got to get to him tonight."

"When do you want to meet?"

Swartz responds, "At 4am, I'll relieve the officers on duty at the hospital. Then I'll go in to finish the job."

Meanwhile, one of Jose's men, who's working as an orderly, calls Jose and says, "Man, I've got good news."

Jose replies, "What's up?"

The orderly informs him, "Mr. Jackson woke up. I overheard the doctor telling a nurse this afternoon."

Jose asks, "Are the cops still outside the door to his room?

"Yes, but one of them got right on his cell phone as soon as he overheard the doctor tell the nurse that Mr. Jackson is speaking."

Jose says, "We don't have much time. I need you to stay low, but keep a close eye on Mr. Jackson. These cops might try to get rid of him tonight. I'll call you back." Jose hangs up with the orderly and calls Ice. "Hey, man, the news is that Mr. Jackson is awake!"

Ice replies, "Good, but those cops are going to try to finish him off before we can talk to him. Are your men still in position?"

Jose says, "Yes."

"Well, keep me updated with that situation. We must keep Mr. Jackson alive at all costs. Tonight's going to be a bad night for someone, but it aint gonna be us!" Ice gets a phone call from Christian.

"Hey, man, what are we going to do about Diamond?"

Ice replies, "The cops have to let her go, they have no choice. She gave a statement, and my lawyer is handling the rest. We'll be fine. I'm keeping her from the club for a few days until we get some more answers."

Christian says, "Any word on Mr. Jackson?"

Ice responds, "Yes, man. You're right on time. Mr. Jackson is awake."

Christian replies, "He is?"

Ice says, "Yeah, man, but you know the dirty agents are going to try to make a move tonight, and we're going to put their lights out."

Christian responds, "I'll tell Peter the goods news!" Christian calls Peter, who is at home eating dinner with his mom. "Peter, you're not going to believe this, Mr. Jackson is awake!"

Peter remains silent for a second then asks, "How long has he been awake?"

Christian replies, "Since sometime after 4pm this afternoon."

Peter says, "We don't have much time. Tell James to hurry up and find out which detectives are at the hospital. I've got to go." Peter hangs up, finishes his meal, and goes to his room. He begins a ninja routine with kicks, punches, and various fighting positions. After a few minutes of sparring, he sits in the middle of the floor and begins to meditate. As he meditates, he thinks of his brother Lim and he wishes he were with him. He jumps up from the floor and performs several catlike jumps. Then he begins preparing the suit with the weapons that will be required to destroy his enemies tonight. Peter exits his house around midnight and speeds off on his motorcycle towards the hospital. His phone buzzes. It's Ice. "I know where you're going, Peter. Don't get hurt, I need you alive."

Peter replies, "Don't worry. My life will not end tonight."

Diamond calls Ice with an update on what's happening at the police station. "Your lawyer Kenneth Bernstein talked to the detectives, and they released me after that. He told me that he would be in touch with me and that I should stay close to home. Then he left."

Ice says, "Ok, but I will have to send someone to get you."

Diamond asks, "What's wrong?"

Ice replies, "Mr. Jackson is conscious now, and I have no word on his protection at the hospital."

Diamond says, "Have you talked to Peter?"

Ice responds, "I did and I'm convinced that he's planning on stopping by the hospital now."

Diamond says, "Please keep me informed. Be careful, honey."

They hang up and Ice calls Christian, "Do you think either you or Victoria can pick up Diamond at the police department?"

Christian replies, "Yes, no problem. Victoria and I will pick her up."

Swartz is driving home. He becomes more and more paranoid as multiple scenarios swirl around in his head. He thinks about Mr. Jackson ratting him out as the shooter in the school as well as the shooter during the heist in Vietnam when they were in the military. There's a good possibility that Jackson could rat him out to the biggest boss over all the crime families in New York, Carlos Columbia, that, for years Swartz has been stealing Carlos' shipments of drugs and selling them at a cheaper market value to the smaller drug lords for side cash. Then Swartz remembers that Mr. Jackson witnessed Swartz rob narcotics from a ship bound for New York years ago that was part of a military seizure. Swartz sold those drugs to a local drug lord for a piece of his business and protection. *All those years, Jackson refused to join us. Swartz says to himself.* "I just can't trust him." Swartz arrives home and his wife has prepared a nice dinner for him.

Susan says, "Did they find the killer on the 96th Street Parkway?"

Swartz replies, "I don't know, we don't have any other witnesses except for that damn girl from the club. She is either lying or hiding something."

She responds "Well, honey, whoever this is, he can't keep this up. Somehow he will slip up. Don't all criminals slip up when they get to greedy?"

Swartz glares at her with an evil look and then takes a drink from his wine glass and smokes his cigarette. His wife wonders about when he is going back out tonight so she can visit her boyfriend who she's having an affair with.

Victoria and Christian pick up Diamond at the police station. Diamond is elated to see them.

Christian asks, "Are you alright, did they put their hands on you?"

She responds, "No, I'm fine, but Peter came to the police station."

Christian says, "He did?"

Diamond replies, "Yes, and he killed some more cops."

Christian says, "Peter has taken this to a whole different level – a level that we didn't expect to be in. I'm glad he is on our side."

They continue to drive to Diamond's house. They get out of the car to go inside the house and they see that someone has broken into the house because the door is wide open. They cautiously enter the house and the place is in shambles.

Victoria screams, "Oh my God! Someone has destroyed my apartment and all the personal items my mother gave me. All the pictures of my family are all cut up on the floor! Who could have done this?!"

Christian replies, "It was Swartz's men, he had them do this!"

Diamond screams, "What can I do, this is not right! I haven't done anything to him. He's tried to rape me and he's sent men to kill me! I can't take this any longer, I'm going to kill him!"

Victoria says, "Calm down, I understand. We all feel bad for you and your boyfriend. He is going to get him for this, you wait and see!"

Back in Hong Kong, Mr. Lim is reading the New York Times and reads about the string of strange police killings in New York. The article reads:

> New York has a strange killer on the loose. A police officer making a routine traffic stop on the 96th Street Parkway was beheaded by a man on a motorcycle with a sword. No evidence left at the scene of the crime. No suspects

*at this time have been identified. The killer came to the police headquarters and killed two policemen. Officer Callahan states that he believes this is the same man who killed the two officers at Mercy Hospital last week. Right now the only clue we have is a card that we believe the killer or sniper leaves at each crime scene.*

Lim, Peter's brother, can't get this out of his mind. He knows from his childhood that it is tradition for ninjas to leave the card at each assassination to warn the next victim. Lim asks himself, "Who could this be? Is it my little brother Peter? Is he in trouble? I must find out."

Back in New York, James has been on the computer all evening and discovers that Swartz has been involved in a few drug-related busts, but the evidence never seems to get to the authorities. Somehow the evidence disappears. But the FBI doesn't have any suspects. Other than that, the biggest drug busts have amounted to small seizers of narcotics and money on several stakeouts operated by Agent Swartz. Somehow the news gets leaked out. James thinks to himself, *That's how he has been getting involved with the mob. He has been doing business with them for years.*

Meanwhile, Swartz prepares to leave. While he's in the shower, Mrs. Swartz emails her boyfriend. The beautiful, sexy, blonde-haired Susan Swartz used to be a professional model before she got into the art business. In her email she asks, *are we still on for the Waldorf Astoria Hotel tonight?* She receives an email response from her boyfriend, Mr. Snow,

*Yes, I will be in New York by 9pm. I should be at the hotel by 11pm and I can't wait to see you.* Susan quickly deletes the email, shuts down the computer, and sips on her wine. She reads her book and waits patiently for Swartz to leave.

Finally, he comes downstairs and he tells her that he received word that Mr. Jackson is awake and he must go to the hospital to protect Mr. Jackson from any return attempts by the killer.

Susan says, "That's good news. But, you be careful." Susan reminisces back to the first time she met Mr. Snow. Mr. Jackson introduced her to Mr. Snow at an art fundraiser held by the Miami Dolphins Charitable Foundation. They were auctioning off art from an art collection, and Susan's art was part of the exhibit on the auction block. Mr. Jackson and Mr. Snow are very close friends.

Swartz kisses Susan on the head and says, "Don't wait up for me tonight, I'm going to be late." And he leaves.

At Diamond's house, the police are conducting their investigation. The detectives are very disrespectful.

One of the officers asks Diamond, "Aren't you the girl who got FBI Agent Rick Waters killed?"

Diamond barks back, "You're a bunch of racist dogs! Get the fuck out of my house! I don't need your help! For all I know, you sorry punks did this to me!"

One of the officers growls back, "You better watch yourself, you little bitch!"

Victoria barks back, "Why, are you going to kill us?!" You guys look like the ones who need to watch out as I see it!"

Ice calls Diamond, "Everything's ok," he says.

She replies, "My place was broken into and the cops just got here, but these motherfuckers are no good!"

Ice responds, "Put the lead cop on the phone." Ice tells the detective, "If anything happens to my girl, your punk ass better not go to sleep tonight!"

The cop slams down the phone, him and his fellow officers exit the scene, and Diamond slams the door.

Meanwhile, it's about 11:30pm, and Susan Swartz is dressed in a black Versace dress with Gucci stiletto shoes. She dresses like a movie star for her boyfriend Mr. Snow. She smiles as she enters the Waldorf Astoria hotel lobby. There he is, dark-haired and handsome, wearing a black double-breasted Albert Kitten suit with black croc Gucci loafers. They meet in the lobby.

"Hi," she says in that sexy, sultry voice.

Mr. Snow kisses her and asks, "Are you hungry?"

She replies, "I'm hungry for you."

They proceed to the hotel restaurant. Mr. Snow tells the waiter to get him the 1979 Pinot Noir red wine. They begin to talk.

Susan says, "I'm becoming very afraid. David's losing it. His coke habit is stressing him way out."

After a sip of wine, Mr. Snow replies, "You should try some, it will calm you down. I heard about Mr. Jackson waking up. I sent flowers and a card to his home. Susan, have you heard anything else about him?"

Susan responds, "David is supposed to be going there tonight."

In a low voice, Mr. Snow asks, "Do they have any leads on the killer?"

Susan replies, "I don't think so, but for some strange reason I don't think that the killer at the hospital was trying to harm Mr. Jackson. If he wanted to kill Mr. Jackson, he certainly could have done it since it was so easy for him to kill all those police officers."

Mr. Snow responds, "You're right, Susan. That is rather strange."

# CHAPTER 6

Back in Hong Kong, Lim is a free man, but he is a fugitive. The search for him is in full force. The corrupt police who are on Chinese mob boss Wo Che Dong's payroll cannot let Lim escape from Hong Kong. If he tells the right authorities, their business ties with the drug cartels in the clothing manufacturing plants around Hong Kong would be in jeopardy. So the most corrupt men in all of China are searching for leads on the whereabouts of Lim. He is hiding out in a small country home right outside Hong Kong City with his girl Tina Zinn.

Tina asks Lim to go out to a small bar for a drink with her.

He replies, "I don't think that's a good idea, I could be seen."

Before they leave, there are three loud knocks at the door. A voice booms through the door, "Open this door! This is the Hong Kong Police Patrol, we've got a missing fugitive prisoner and we need everyone in the neighborhood to be extremely careful! The fugitive is armed and dangerous."

Tina talks through the door, "I live here alone!"

The Chinese policeman yells back, "I must search your home!"

As Lim hides in the house, Tina opens the door and allows the cop in. The Chinese detective glances around, but he doesn't see anything.

He looks down at the kitchen table, "Why do you have your table set for two people, but you say you live here alone?"

Tina replies, "I always keep it that way, I might get lucky and meet someone like you, sir."

The policeman smiles at her and asks, "What do you have to eat?"

She says, "I have some herbal tea and chicken noodle soup."

He accepts, "I'll have some." He sits down to eat. He says, "I bet you could give me a wonderful time, he he he." And smiles at Tina in a perverted manner. After he's finished eating the soup, he says, "Come over here and take your clothes off." Then he begins to pull on Tina.

Infuriated, Lim sneaks from behind the curtain and says, "You're looking for a good time? I will give you one straight to hell where you belong!"

The surprised officer yells back, "I'll kill you."

As he pulls out his gun, Lim pulls out his ninja sword and slices off the cop's hand. As the cop screams in pain, Lim whips out the rope he used to escape from prison, loops it around the screaming cop's neck, and strangles him to death.

Once the cop's body stops twitching on the ground and

goes limp, Tina screams, "Oh my God! What are we going to do with him?"

Lim replies, "We'll take his clothes off and I'll get rid of the body."

The terrified Tina begins to cry and sob.

Lim comforts her, "I won't let anyone harm you. You're all I have right now. We must be strong. We made it this far. We must not allow fear to stop us. Lim embraces and kisses her. Lim then removes the dead policeman's body to the woods behind the back of the house, finds a good burial spot, and commences to dig a grave and buries the body.

When he finishes and returns to the house, Tina worriedly says, "The police are searching everywhere for you. It's not safe for you to leave."

As she's speaking, Lim has an idea. He says, "Bring me the cop's uniform." Lim tries on the uniform with the shoes, and everything fits perfectly.

Tina says, "I understand. You can disguise yourself as a cop. What are we going to do with his gun?"

Lim responds, "If I'm going to be a police officer, I must have a gun. But, don't worry, Tina, I don't need guns."

Swartz gets a phone call from one of the agents tailing his wife. The agent says, "I just got word your wife was seen in the restaurant at the Waldorf Astoria with Mr. Snow. Do you want me to do anything?"

Swartz replies, "No, I've got plans for them when we get to Colorado!"

The agent says, "Ok, Boss."

Swartz replies, "Thank you."

Meanwhile, James calls Ice, "Hey, Ice, I got some news you're not going to believe!"

Ice replies, "What do you got?"

James says, "Mr. Snow and Swartz's wife are having dinner at the restaurant at the Waldorf Astoria."

Ice responds in disbelief, "You're kidding."

James says, "No, I'm dead serious. I think Swartz has a trail on her and he knows about it. I also overhead the officer's come inside Swartz's house and put a phone call into an agent when she rolled out."

Ice replies, "Wow! Mrs. Swartz could be the next one to get killed!"

James asks, "What should we do? We must tell Christian about his dad!"

Ice replies, "Yes, we should. His father's definitely in danger. This is a problem that we must prevent! James, call Jose and let him know what's going on and tell him to send me a man to watch Mr. Snow until we figure out what we must do about this."

James calls Jose and updates him about the situation.

Jose says, "No problem, but what about our man Christian?"

James replies, "I don't think we should call Christian yet. Let's wait for Ice to give us the word on this."

At the restaurant in the Waldorf Astoria Hotel, sitting across the room from Mr. Snow and Susan Swartz is Jimmy "The Fox" Marchetti, who's having dinner with his wife. Mr. Snow and Susan don't see The Fox, but he sees them. He walks over to their table.

"What a surprise to see you here, Snow!"

Mr. Snow replies, "It's good to see you, Mr. Marchetti."

The Fox turns to Susan, "Susan, how are you? I've been meaning to ask you how the art business is going."

As she begins to speak, Mr. Snow wants to interrupt her, but she kicks him underneath the table and says, "I'm glad you asked. Mr. Snow flew into New York last minute to give me some last minute details on my upcoming art exhibit that is being held at his restaurant in Colorado."

Mr. Marchetti replies, "That's great. I wish you much success!" He looks to Mr. Snow, "How long are you in town for?"

Mr. Snow replies, "I fly back to Miami in the morning."

Mr. Marchetti says, "Well, I don't want your food to get cold. Try the cannolis, they're very good here."

Mr. Snow replies, "Thanks, I will."

Mr. Marchetti says, "Goodbye."

Mr. Snow replies, "Goodbye."

Susan Swartz says to Mr. Snow, "You know Mr. Marchetti?"

Mr. Snow answers, "Yes, I did some business with him in New York."

Susan replies, "I don't like him. David says he is the biggest crime lord in New York."

Mr. Snow retorts, "He isn't the biggest, but he thinks he is, that arrogant son of a bitch. But you did good, don't worry."

Mr. Marchetti calls Swartz and says "Did you know your wife is having an affair with Mr. Snow?" He sarcastically continues, "Don't answer that, I forgot, you FBI agents have intel on everyone, even your wives. Have a good evening, David."

Swartz becomes infuriated. He says to himself, "This motherfucker thinks I'm some kind of a dumb ass. I will kill you, Fox. Just wait and see, you Italian bastard!"

In the meantime, Christian, Victoria, and Diamond go out to get something to eat.

Diamond says, "I'm glad you're with me."

Victoria replies, "That's what friends are for."

They drive down to Canal Street in Chinatown.

Diamond says, "I love Chinese food."

They go into The Big Wong Chinese restaurant, sit down in a booth towards the back of the restaurant, and order their food. In the booth directly behind them, two men are conversing in Chinese. Victoria, who is currently studying Chinese in school, is intently listening to their conversation. She tells everyone at their table what is being said between the two men in the booth behind them.

"There was a prisoner who broke out of a Chinese prison and he killed a number of correctional officers during the escape. One of the guards killed during the escape was related to the cook in the restaurant. He was his brother. One of the men says that the prisoner is still at large as a fugitive in Hong Kong. It's been a week since the escape and there's been no sightings of the convict. The fugitive is a dangerous killer."

Then one of the men gets up from the table and goes into the back kitchen of the restaurant.

Victoria says, "I could hear the fear in their voices. The escaped prisoner in China must be a real bad-ass killer. There's only one concern those guys have, one of them said 'If this man finds his false accusers of the crime he did not commit, this could change the business here at the restaurant.'"

It's about 3am, Peter's in the men's bathroom at the hospital, which is right next to Mr. Jackson's room. He hears an FBI agent speaking with the police outside Jackson's door.

"Swartz wants to speak with Mr. Jackson."

A nurse calls Doctor Mitchell, the head physician, to the hallway outside Mr. Jackson's room, "These police are trying to go into Mr. Jackson's room."

Dr. Mitchell says, "Swartz, I don't think this is an appropriate time to speak to Mr. Jackson. He is finally getting some rest."

Swartz replies, "I need to know if he remembers the shooter. This is the only way I can help him."

Dr. Mitchell concedes, "Alright, but make it quick." Dr. Mitchell leaves, and Swartz enters Mr. Jackson's room with Agent Smith. There are a few more officers outside the door.

Swartz says, "Hello, Jackson."

In a low, raspy voice, Mr. Jackson replies, "Hello, David."

Swartz gets close to Mr. Jackson's ear and whispers, "I know you understand why I'm here."

Mr. Jackson listens. Meanwhile, Peter comes out of the bathroom. He sneaks past the nurse standing in the hallway and throws a tranquilizer dart at the first police officer. As he falls down, Peter sneaks up behind the second police officer who's drinking a cup of coffee and breaks his neck. Peter enters Mr. Jackson's room. When the agents see Peter, they attempt to pull their weapons. Peter hurls shurikens at both Swartz and Agent Smith, however, the shurikens don't kill either man. Smith is hit in the arm and Swartz is hit in the chest. The force of the shurikens knock both men to the floor. As both men lie stunned on the floor, Peter grabs Agent Smith's handcuffs and cuffs him to the bed. Swartz gets his wits about him and tries again for his gun. Peter whips a dart into Swartz's neck and he passes out, but he doesn't die. He whips out his samurai sword and plunges it into Agent Smith's chest.

Mr. Jackson pleads with Peter, "Please don't kill me!"

Peter calmly replies, "I won't hurt you, just get better. You're like a father to me."

Jackson recognizes the voice from the shadowy figure, "Peter, is that you!?"

Peter leaves.

Mr. Jackson calls for the nurse.

She enters and upon seeing the dead FBI agents she screams, "Are you okay? How badly are you hurt?"

Mr. Jackson replies, "I'm fine, but get me out of this room."

Dr. Mitchell enters the room. He can't believe Mr. Jackson is alive. They call the police and immediately move Mr. Jackson to another room with no room number to ensure his safety.

Ice's boys call Ice and tell him what's happened. They tell him, "This killer is no joke! He can't be stopped! The doctor and nurse moved Mr. Jackson to an undisclosed room, but we'll find out where he is."

Ice replies, "Thanks guys. I'll talk to you soon. Stay in touch. Our only help is Mr. Jackson, and he understands now that his life is in danger."

The police arrive at the hospital. Swartz has a deep cut in his chest that requires several stitches. Agent Smith is dead from a puncture to his heart. Homicide detective William Sanders is the lead detective onsite. He is one of the few honest cops who was a big fan of Mr. Jackson's NFL career. He has been following the case since the first killing at the hospital.

He begins to question Swartz, "Did you see the killer?"

Swartz says, "Of course, I saw him! You think I inflicted harm to my own body? Of course, I saw him!"

Mr. Sanders replies, "I understand your anger, but I'm here to solve this case and protect you. Whoever this was, he didn't spare you for nothing. He definitely could have killed you."

Swartz responds, "This guy had a black mask on and was wearing a black leather bodysuit. This guy moved so fast, it appeared sometimes as if there were two of them."

The other homicide detective finds two ninja cards on the floor beside the wall of the room. "Hey, I found something."

Mr. Sanders looks at them and says, "Have we found where these cards have originated from?"

The second detective says, "We are still waiting for that information."

Swartz asks, "Is Mr. Jackson alright?"

Detective Sanders replies, "Yes, we moved him to another room."

Swartz says, "Give me his new room number and I will get my agents to secure the area."

Mr. Sanders replies, "This is now a New York City

Police high-profile homicide case. It's my job now to ensure that the utmost level of security and witness protection are underway.

Later that day, Dr. Mitchell calls Mr. Jackson's daughter Tonya, "Your father is in danger. There was another shooting at the hospital and your father definitely saw the killer this time. The killer never harmed your father, though he killed three more cops. Don't worry, Tonya, I've moved him to another room."

Tonya replies, "Thank you, Dr. Mitchell. Can I talk to him?"

Dr. Mitchell says, "Let me get him safely to another part of the hospital and I will give you his room number and phone number."

Tonya responds, "Thanks, Dr. Mitchell."

Dr. Mitchell replies, "No problem, Tonya. Let's stay in touch. See you tomorrow."

The next day, Swartz returns home.

His wife is very concerned about him, "Can I get you anything?"

Swartz replies, "Get me a scotch on the rocks."

After she retrieves him the drink, she asks, "Have you spoken with Smith's wife Diane yet? She is very grief stricken."

Swartz responds, "I will be seeing her tomorrow at the press meeting." Swartz asks, "Where were you last night?"

She replies, "I had a last minute meeting with someone regarding my art show in Colorado later this month."

Swartz growls, "Stop lying to me! You more or less went on a dinner date with Mr. Snow!"

Susan fires back, "That's what you think!"

Swartz yells, "Yeah, you think I'm stupid or something!? Your ass is fucking around on me, aren't you!" and Swartz smacks her in the mouth.

Susan, shocked with tears welling up in her eyes, screams, "You sick bastard! You're drunk and high on coke! Don't EVER hit me again, you asshole! GET OUT!"

Swartz screams back, "You can't put me out, Bitch! YOU get out!"

She screams back, "I WILL!!"

Swartz, feeling guilty about the slap, apologetically says, "Wait, I'm sorry, don't leave."

Susan screams, "You WILL be SORRY!" throws a lamp at Swartz's head, runs out the front door, and slams it with a loud BANG!

Swartz runs out the front door as Susan gets in her Mercedes truck. She peels out of the driveway, and Swartz hurls a flower pot that was sitting on the porch at her vehicle with all his might, but misses. The cops who were assigned to protect her that were sitting in front of the house start up the engine of their squad car and follow her.

One of the police officers stays back with Swartz and says, "Calm down, man."

Swartz goes back inside and resumes drinking, smoking, and snorting lines of cocaine.

On the road, the frantic, shaken Susan phones Mr. Snow.

Mr. Snow says, "Hello, Susan."

She cries, "I'm sorry to call you so early in the morning,

but David is going crazy. He just hit me and is accusing me of sleeping with you."

Mr. Snow replies, "That's not good. Where are you now?"

Crying, Susan says, "I'm going over to my sister Debbie's house."

Mr. Snow tells her, "You stay there and stay away from David. He's going mad and that could be dangerous for both of us. But try to stay calm and call me when you reach your sister's house."

Susan promises, "Ok, I love you."

Mr. Snow replies, "I love you, too. Goodbye."

CHAPTER 7

In Hong Kong, Lim reads in the local Chinese newspaper:

*Killer strikes again at New York's Mercy Hospital. Three more officers killed ninja style. The two witnesses were FBI Agent David Swartz and patient Mr. Jackson, who survived. The description of the killer is a man about 5' 8", 150 pounds. The report also says the same ninja cards left at the crime scene were the same type of cards left at the other two crime scenes. Detectives from the New York City Homicide Department are still trying to apprehend the assailant. There's no further information at this time.*

Lim says, "I must go to New York."

Tina replies, "You will be caught. Do you want to go back to prison and spend the rest of your life there?"

Lim says, "I must help my brother."

Tina asks, "How are you so sure it's him?"

Lim replies, "The cards, if I'm correct, are from my

ancestor's lineage. Only a few families from China would have such an ancient card from the 1800s. My family has ties to one of the first ninja families."

Tina says, "Ok, but how do you expect to travel to New York?"

Lim replies, "Tina, I have been giving this a lot of thought. I think I can catch a cargo boat full of products to be sold in New York.

Tina asks, "How soon do you plan on leaving?"

Lim says, "I need you to get me some money, a map of New York, and a cell phone. When I have these items, I should be ready to board a boat."

The press conference regarding the new killings is now being held at the Mercy Hospital conference room.

Lead Detective Sanders begins, "As of yesterday, on behalf of the New York City Police Department, we have put this case on a state-wide high-priority crime alert status with further cooperation from the Rhode Island State Police, the local Long Island Police Department, the Staten Island Police Department, and all the local New Jersey State police departments. Right now we have four police officers and one secret FBI Agent killed within the last few days, and the only evidence we have are the oriental calling cards left by the killer and a brief description of the assailant. As we get more information, we will provide it to the media and general public. This police investigation falls under the jurisdiction of the New York City Police Department and we've just provided all the information that we're allowed under these conditions. If there are any questions, I now open the floor to you. Go ahead.

Ed Young, from TV 7 News starts, "Detective Sanders, do you think there is some kind of conspiracy threat to the New York City Police Department?"

Sanders answers, "We are not sure who or how many are involved with these killings. It's still too early to come to these conclusions." Detective Sanders then points to Mike Taylor of CNN News who asks, "The young woman that was stopped on the 96th Street Parkway…do we know why she was stopped and did this woman know the killer somehow?"

Detective Sanders answers, "That's a good question. She has been questioned. Right now she remains a witness to a murder and will be in touch with her lawyer as we get more details on the case. Well, everyone, my time is up and we've got a lot of investigating to do and information to gather. Thank you for your time. If you have any information regarding the case, please call 1-800-NYC-NYPD or visit the crime stoppers section of the police's website at www.nypd.com.

Back at the high school, Principal Hamlin calls a school-wide assembly at the auditorium. All the boys are present.

Principal Hamlin introduces Detective Sanders to the school, "Kids, since the city has a killer on the loose, I felt that our school could use some insight and assurance from Detective William Sanders, the chief detective of the New York City Police Department."

Mr. Sanders nods and begins, "Kids, I understand your concern, especially with Mr. Jackson being wounded by the killer, he's still in the hospital, and the killer is still at large in the city. Mr. Jackson is a longtime friend of mine.

We go way back to his playing days in the NFL. There's no other person that I care more about than Mr. Jackson. I will, personally do WHATEVER it takes to find the shooter and killer. Once again, we want you to call us if you find ANY information on these incidents. We must help each other. Remember, there is safety in numbers. If we all work together we can solve this problem. Thank you, students of Mount Saint Mary High School!"

The kids in the school like Detective Sanders. They appreciate his sincerity and erupt in thunderous applause and cheers. The boys' new science teacher is named Richard Wyatt. He comes from a school in Brooklyn.

He starts off the class, "I understand your love for Mr. Jackson, but I can't be him. I will try my best to help you keep some fun in science class and will do my best to make sure that you all remain outstanding students."

Peter walks into class late.

Mr. Wyatt says, "So, who are you, sir?"

Peter replies, "I'm Peter," and sits down at an empty desk.

Mr. Wyatt asks, "Why are you so late?"

Peter responds, "My sister is in the hospital sick with terminal cancer and my mother couldn't be with her this morning."

Mr. Wyatt says, "Oh, ok, I'm sorry to hear that."

A voice from the back of the class yells out, "What? She eat some rat poison!?" The bully's name is Robert Finnegan. He's about 6'2" and 210 pounds, a tall white boy who's the varsity football team's star quarterback. He's very cocky and conceited.

Shocked and appalled, Mr. Wyatt asks Robert, "Why would you say something like that?"

Robert responds, "Don't all Chinese people eat rats?!",

Mr. Wyatt barks at him, "That is a very racist comment and I WON'T have that in my class! I'm sure Mr. Jackson wouldn't have allowed a comment like that, and I CERTAINLY WON'T allow a comment like that either so you apologize NOW for what you said!"

Robert arrogantly snickers, "If that Chinese boy got a problem, he's got a mouth too. He can use it!"

Peter says calmly, "Words don't hurt me. What you don't understand could hurt you, so choose your words wisely."

Robert says, "I got your understanding, you Chinese piece of shit. Anytime, you want me, boy, I'm here."

Mr. Wyatt steps in and says, "Ok, Robert, that's enough! If you keep disrupting my class you will have to go to the principal's office!"

After class, the boys go to the cafeteria.

At the lunch table, Ice says to Peter, "I like the way you handled things in science class."

Peter replies, "We don't need any homicides in school."

James says, "You know, that guy Robert is the star football player at this school and his dad plays golf with Swartz. Robert is also running for class president."

Christian says to James, "Robert's the school bully, that's all. Neither he nor his father are a threat to us right now."

Jose chimes in, "I have one problem – this guy tried to punk Peter, and if Peter keeps avoiding him, he will try to do something to get Peter's attention and that could get Robert hurt."

Ice says, "Doesn't that guy eat lunch at this period."

Christian replies, "Yes, he does."

Ice says, "So, if I see him, I'll speak with him."

While they're all eating their lunch at the table, Robert approaches the table, says, "Hi, guys!" and spits in Peter's food.

Ice barks at him, "Wow! Man, you are JUST CRAZY!"

Robert replies to Ice, "Well, your friend Peter told me to choose my words wisely, so I spit instead of wasting time trying to choose my words wisely!"

Peter gets up from his seat, walks around the table, and calmly gets in Robert's face. He says to Robert, "Did you not fully understand what I said to you?"

Robert sarcastically remarks, "I guess I didn't understand. But you understand that I spit in your food." Ice and Christian stand up an attempt to physically separate Peter and Robert, but Peter quickly flips around to Robert's back, grabs Robert's hands, and puts them in a hold behind his back. He calmly says to Robert, "Get me another plate of food." He walks the struggling Robert over to the food line, squeezing Robert's hands with a painful force that Robert's never felt. Peter whispers into Robert's ear, "Don't ever speak to me like that again because if you do you'll be needing to fit your limbs in a prosthesis and your football career will be nothing short of a fan watching from the stands. Understand?"

Robert, wincing in pain, whimpers under his breath, "Yes." Robert walks Peter's new tray of food over to the lunch table and puts it down. He walks away embarrassed with his head down in shame.

Ice says, "I'm glad you didn't hurt him, Peter. He's not an enemy, just a problem."

Susan Swartz arrives at her sister Debbie's house, who is glad to see her. When they greet, they hold each other for a long time. Susan's parents both died in a tragic plane crash when Susan was a little girl. Debbie's married with two kids named Wendy and Bradley Jr. Her husband is Brad Nelson, a construction foreman supervisor for Winn Constructions Developers, one of the biggest developers in the state of New York.

The kids see their Auntie Susan and they run to her with excitement, jump on her, and says, "We missed you! Did you bring any of your artwork with you?"

Aunt Susan replies, "No, but if you're good, we can do some art together!"

The kids love it when their Aunt Susan paints for them. Little Brad says he wants to be an artist one day.

Debbie asks Susan, "Are you hungry?"

Susan replies, "I'm starved."

Debbie says, "Hold on, I will get you something to eat. Brad's working the late-night shifts this week at the Manhattan Bridge, so dinner is ready now."

They begin eating, and Debbie looks to Susan, "What's really going on?"

Susan replies, "David is in financial trouble. I can't keep borrowing money to cover our expenses. David has maxed out our credit cards, and the mortgage on the New Jersey home is two months behind."

Debbie asks, "Is your artwork helping you get through this?"

Susan replies, "No, not really."

Debbie says, "Then who are you getting money from?"

Susan becomes awkwardly silent and begins to cry. "I'm sorry, Debbie. But David and I are almost finished. I don't love him."

Debbie asks, "What are you trying to say?"

After a long pause, Susan finally answers, "I'm seeing Mr. Snow, and he's helping me pay our bills."

Debbie replies, "But that's one of David's old friends!"

Susan replies, "Yes, but I'm in love with him. I don't know what to do."

Debbie asks, "Isn't he still married?"

Susan replies, "Yes, but she is never in the country because she travels a lot because of her shoe line out of Milan, Italy."

The concerned Debbie says, "Sister, this is very risky. You could really hurt your business or your relationship with Snow, not to mention if David finds out the truth he would kill you. You remember how jealous he is."

Susan says, "I don't care. I've got to be happy, and I've felt the happiest in my life with the little time that I've shared with this man."

Debbie replies, "Of course, I understand, Susan, and I will always be in your corner. All we have is each other. I love you."

Susan responds, "I love you, too."

They continue eating and enjoying their dinner.

After school, the boys are out in the parking lot getting

ready to drive home. Some members of the football team walk over.

The 6' 5" nose tackle named Lorenzo Alexander says, "You punks got a problem or something? No one puts their hands on our family!"

Ice replies, "What family are you talking about? Your family at home that your punk ass needs to run home to or the family that you are ready to die for that hasn't won a state championship in two years?!"

Lorenzo taunts, "You gotta lot of mouth for a sorry rapper like your father!"

The members of the football team surround Ice. James and Christian get out of their cars. Jose and Peter had already left the school. Lorenzo gets in Ice's face and punches Ice in the face. Christian jumps in while James calls Peter. After Christian jumps in, the football players turn their attention towards him. James tries to stop them, but he gets pushed to the ground. The school security guards run over and break up the melee. The football players go to the locker room to get ready for practice. After practice, the teams return to the locker room to shower and go home, but they meet an uninvited guest – it's Peter, he's dressed in his black leather body suit along with his black mask. His black leather gloves sport the red grips on the fingers and the black boots have the red soles. His black utility belt carries every weapon that a ninja assassin would require.

In shock, one of the football players says, "This could be the killer!"

Peter replies, "I want the dudes that were involved in the fight in the parking lot earlier today to step forward!"

Robert the quarterback says, "We ain't doing nothing you ask for, Halloween punk!"

Peter asks them again, "I'm going to say this one more time, if you don't cooperate, I'm going to have to find out for myself!" Peter kicks one of the football players, who still has his helmet on, in the helmet. It flies off and hits the wall. *Boom!* The players drop to the floor. Peter asks, "Do the rest of you want to be treated like this?"

Lorenzo Alexander attempts to tackle Peter, but Peter punches him in the stomach. Lorenzo vomits violently. Peter kicks Lorenzo in the head and Lorenzo drops to the floor. *Boom!*

The other players plead with Peter, "It wasn't me!"

Robert Finnegan claims, "I'm not scared of no wanna be ninja, I got a baseball bat and my helmet's on, I got your ninja! But you gotta be ready for some football with a Yankee baseball bat, you stupid bastard!"

As Robert picks up the bat, Peter quickly takes out his sword and slices the bat in two. Robert throws the one half of the bat at Peter, but Peter catches it and breaks it with his knee and then kicks Robert's helmet off his head.

Peter calmly says, "Let this be a warning to you! If you ever touch my friends again you will never play football again, let this be the final warning!"

The rest of the players run to the exit to attempt to get out of the locker room, but Peter had locked the door. Peter quickly exited the locker room through a small window over the ventilation system. The janitor hears the football players banging on the door, and he unlocks the door to let them out.

CHAPTER 8

It's Saturday. Tonya flies to New York and takes a taxicab from the airport to visit her father in the hospital. Upon her arrival, she is greeted by Dr. Mitchell, his staff, and two policeman to escort her to Mr. Jackson's room. Two other men appear at the scene who identify themselves as policemen, but they're not. They explain that there's been a change in plans – the FBI has taken over and that they are taking Mr. Jackson to a private facility for his protection.

Dr. Mitchell says, "But Detective Sanders of the New York City Police Department is in charge of the case."

FBI Agent Tom Reynolds replies, "But he's got no jurisdiction in this matter. We deal with protective custody for patients with tight security measures. This man is in danger and we have to step in. I assure you that Detective Sanders has been notified, and we have his cooperation. It's in Mr. Jackson's best interest."

FBI Agent Reynolds and his partner enter into Mr. Jackson's new room - #B12. Mr. Jackson's asleep.

Tonya asks, "Can I have a word with my father before he is moved?"

The FBI Agent replies, "Ok, but don't take too long," and they exit.

She softly says, "Daddy, it's me. I love you, Daddy. I've been praying for you all day."

Mr. Jackson, now awake, replies, "Baby, you're in danger."

Tonya says, "What's going on?"

Mr. Jackson begins to say, "Swartz–" but is interrupted by the two FBI agents who reenter the room and tell Tonya that she must leave.

Agent Reynolds says, "Mr. Jackson, it's time to leave."

Mr. Jackson asks, "Who are you? And where is Detective Sanders?"

The agent replies, "He has been informed that we've taken over your security detail, but we must move you to a safer facility quickly. Our intel has told us that the killers are planning to finish the job of killing you tonight."

Mr. Jackson remains quiet. He leaves a note for Tonya under the bed. After the agents remove Mr. Jackson from the room, Tonya reenters the room where her father was, she remembers the short words her father said, and she has no doubt something is wrong. She looks around the room and finds the note from her dad which says, *Tonya, I love you, 1 Peter 5:7 Casting all your cares upon him for he careth for you.* Tonya realizes there's more to this message than what first appears. She remembers the student in her science class named Peter who her father was very fond of. She thinks that this could be the Peter that her dad referenced in the note.

James calls Ice. "There's been a change. The FBI has

given some false information to Dr. Mitchell. They're taking Mr. Jackson to a warehouse in SoHo Chinatown to question him and then kill him!"

Ice screams, "You tell Jose to get my boys over there now!" Ice hangs up with James and calls Peter.

Peter answers, "What's up?"

Ice tells him, "Swartz's men have taken Mr. Jackson out of the hospital and transporting him to a warehouse in SoHo Chinatown called the Chan Wing House." Ice continues, "Listen, Peter, we need Mr. Jackson alive."

Peter replies, "Call Detective Sanders because I'm going to get them before they reach SoHo. Did they take him by car or ambulance?"

Ice says, "By ambulance, and once they arrive in the SoHo neighborhood, they're going to switch to an unmarked car to take him into the warehouse. That's what James found out."

Peter responds, "Have Detective Sanders meet me at the warehouse. I will call you after I've caught up with Mr. Jackson's ambulance." Peter leaves the restaurant he was having lunch at in Chinatown and jumps on his Ducati bike and speeds down Canal Street until he hits the parkway. As he's driving, his phone buzzes. It's James.

James says, "The ambulance with Mr. Jackson is at the Manhattan Tunnel (which is 3 exits away from the Canal Street exit).

Peter replies, "No problem, I'm close. The ambulance is in my sight." Peter drives up behind the ambulance and jumps onto the back of the ambulance from his bike. His bike runs into a fence guard rail. Peter busts open the back door of the ambulance. He kicks one agent out of the ambulance onto the street. The agent is hit by a cab driver and he's knocked across the highway.

Agent Reynolds pulls his weapon and fires it at Peter, but he misses him. Peter hurls a shuriken and hits Reynolds right between the eyes. The driver brings the ambulance to a screeching halt.

Peter tells Mr. Jackson, "Don't worry, you're safe now."

Another officer got out of the front seat of the ambulance and attempted to sneak up on Peter from behind. Peter throws a shuriken at the agent's hand holding the drawn firearm. The man fires a shot, but misses Peter. Peter takes out his sword and cuts the agent's throat. Peter sprints back to his motorcycle and speeds off. By that time, the NYPD have received the call about the accident in the Manhattan tunnel.

Ice calls Peter. "Detective Sanders is on his way to the ambulance."

Peter replies, "Ok." Peter then jumps the curb over the highway, drives down it on the opposite side of the road, and leaves the area.

The police spot him and put an APB out to all the police in the vicinity, but Peter's high performance motorcycle is too quick for the police vehicles. The police advise each other, "Don't pursue the motorcycle guy, we could cost some innocent people their lives with a high-speed chase. The NYPD arrive at the ambulance, and Detective Sanders finds Mr. Jackson breathing very heavily and in a state of shock. The police on the scene also find the dead agents with two more ninja cards placed on their bodies including Agent Reynolds, who still has the samurai sword sticking out of his head. They transport Mr. Jackson back to Mercy Hospital. Detective Sanders calls Dr. Mitchell to let him know they are en route with Mr. Jackson.

He tells Dr. Mitchell, "Let Mr. Jackson's daughter know that he is okay."

At the crime scene, the NYPD put yellow crime scene caution tape around the borders of the scene. Their detectives begin their investigation. They discover that the last guy that was killed was cut at close range judging from the distance between the bullet holes on the ambulance door and the casings on the ground.

Detective Jerry Edwards says, "This was not an attack on Mr. Jackson, but on the FBI agents who were transporting Mr. Jackson in the ambulance. The killer knew where they were going and when they would be at the Manhattan Tunnel. The killer definitely has outside help. But we have a problem with our FBI Agency. There's a problem somewhere."

Swartz shows up at the crime scene.

Detective Edwards shows him around and asks, "Do you know who could have given the order from your agency to change the location for Mr. Jackson's safety?"

Swartz replies with a glare at Edwards, "I'm not sure. We've put our agency on top priority code red because of all the recent deaths. There's a breach of security and intel. But to answer your question as to who gave the order, only the dead agents would know or there is some kind of setup in place to kill police officers and FBI agents. This could be the work of a new Al Qaeda group who's frustrated with the U.S. When I find the source, we'll expose and destroy it."

Edwards replies, "Did you know these men?"

Swartz responds, "Yes, but they wouldn't have moved Mr. Jackson unless another superior senior agent gave them instructions."

Edwards says, "Well, I must get this crime scene cleaned up."

Swartz replies, "I understand." Swartz leaves the crime scene and is furious. He just left the bodies of his best friend Agent Reynolds along with the bodies of two other agents. He drives to the same restaurant in Chinatown where Victoria, Christian, and Diamond were eating dinner. He enters The Big Wong restaurant and asks a waiter, "Is Mr. Wang available?"

The waiter inquires, "Can I ask who you are so I can let him know?"

Swartz replies, "Tell him it's Swartz."

The waiter runs upstairs to Mr. Wang's office and pokes his head in the door, "A Mr. Swartz is here to see you."

Mr. Wang responds, "Send him upstairs to my office."

Swartz walks upstairs and knocks on the door to Mr. Wang's private office.

"Come in," says Wang, "I've been expecting you."

Swartz enters and sits down.

"I've read recently about your agents getting killed in a very unusual manner."

Swartz replies, "Yes, do you know anyone who could be capable of doing such highly skilled killings?"

Wang says, "The Wo Tang Chi Gang have such special

skills, but they don't kill unless there's drugs and money involved."

Swartz replies, "Then who could have done this?"

Wang says, "The only family that would be able to perform such high-skilled killings as these would be descendants of true ancient ninja warriors. My family has only read about this, but I have never met anyone with these types of skills. This type could only come from the farmlands of Hong Kong."

Swartz replies, "Has your business been productive?"

Wang responds, "Yes. I thank you for your protection. I have an envelope at the front desk in the restaurant for you, Swartz."

Swartz replies, "If you hear anything about this ninja warrior, could you call me?"

Wang says, "Yes, I will call you with any information I get."

Swartz retrieves his envelope and leaves. He opens the envelope. In it was $10,000 dollars and a note that says: *Swartz, we have a very unique problem. You tell me that this killer is a threat to you and our operation. If it is, indeed, a ninja warrior, he will not stop until he kills you. You must stop him before he stops you. Someone you know has your answer, Mr. Swartz. Please do not come back to the restaurant. Whoever is associated with you will die also. – Mr. Wang*

Inside the restaurant, Mr. Wang calls for a meeting with his family. He says, "We have a problem. Lim has escaped from prison in China, and he could be heading for the U.S. Our boss Mr. Wo Che-Pong has told me that the drugs coming in from Hong Kong are safe, but there is still danger. Our greatest concern is Lim going back to the manufacturing plant that his family still owns. This would be a problem. I'm sending my son Daniel to find Lim and stop him before he stops us. He leaves for Hong Kong tomorrow. The rest of you need to find this killer or copycat ninja we have in New York. If he is a family member of Lim, we need to kill him. Lim has a younger brother. I want Gerald to visit him at his house and find out if he has the skills to fight like a ninja. Gerald knows how to test him.

"Yes, sir," Gerald replies, "I'll do this."

Mr. Wang says to Gerald, "I want you to go tonight. Gerald drives to Peter's house and knocks on the door.

Mrs. Wong answers, "Yes, can I help you?"

Gerald says, "Is Peter home?"

Mrs. Wong says, "No, who are you?"

Gerald replies, "I'm a friend of Peter and his father. My uncle wants to invite him to our party at the Big Wong restaurant.

Peter's Mom says, "Peter went to St. John's Hospital to visit his sister. She is sick with cancer."

Gerald replies, "I'm so sorry to hear that. Well, tell him I stopped by."

Mrs. Wong responds, "No problem."

Gerald then drives to St. John's Hospital. Peter's sister Jenny is very sick. Gerald finds her room and begins to open the door. Peter hears the door knob and quickly hides behind the door. Gerald enters the room and walks over to the bed where Jenny is asleep. Peter pulls out his sword and puts it behind his back as Gerald turns around to leave.

Peters asks, "Can I help you?"

Gerald asks, "Are you Peter Wong?"

Peter replies, "Who's asking?"

Gerald says, "I mean you no harm. I'm Gerald. My uncle owns the Big Wong restaurant, and we would like you to come next Saturday."

As Gerald walks to the door, Gerald tries to drop the soda bottle that he was drinking into the trash can by the door, but he purposely misses to see if Peter has the reflexes of a ninja fighting expert. As the bottle drops behind the trash can, Peter kicks the bottle back up to his hand like a professional soccer player.

Gerald says, "I'm sorry. Thanks for catching that soda, it would have woken your sister up. Where did you learn that trick?"

Peter replies, "I played soccer in middle school."

In Hong Kong, Lim, wearing his police uniform, is at his parents' clothing manufacturing plant. It's 2 am. There are still some employees and security guards at the factory. Lim slides in through the back door by the loading area where there is about 15 trucks. One of the Chinese employees asks, "Can I help you, officer?"

Lim replies, "I'm just checking the security system."

The worker responds, "You wait right here, I'll need the supervisor to meet you."

Lim says, "No, first come here, I need to show you something."

As the worker approaches Lim, Lim takes out his rope and loops it around the worker's neck and strangles him to death. He pulls the worker's dead body behind the truck and puts it into the dumpster. Lim then makes his way back into the warehouse and walks up some steps that lead to a door with a sign that says *Top Security Clearance Personnel Only*. Lim breaks into the room and finds wooden boxes of cloths with silver foil bags in them. He begins to investigate through the unfamiliar bags when he hears two men outside say, "Hey, the door is broken. Whoever's in there, they'll never be able to get out. Get your guns out." They enter the room. Lim is hiding under a cutting table as the men search the room.

One of the men says, "Turn the lights on."

As the other man turns on the light, Lim hurls a dart at him that puts him to sleep instantly.

The first guard yells, "Hey, who are you!?"

Lim whips a knife and it pierces the man's chest and lungs. He dies instantly. Lim leaves the room, but brings a silver foil bag with him. More men enter the back area looking for the two men. Lim sprints for the back exit. The security guards see him and fire their weapons at him, but they miss. As Lim leaps over the fence, he whips his shuriken at an officer, it pierces the man's neck and the man instantly dies.

Meanwhile, Daniel is at home preparing for his early-morning flight to Hong Kong when he receives a call from his father Mr. Wang. "Son, we have just received news that Lim has entered the warehouse in Hong Kong. We must stop him before it's too late."

"Ice is in trouble," James says to Ice's dad, "I found out that the FBI set up an illegal search of your home. They possibly went into the apartment and planted drugs there to set you up, sir!"

His father says, "What? Who did this?"

James says, "Swartz, the FBI agent."

He responds, "How did you get this information?"

James replies, "I can't tell you that right now, sir. Please help Ice. He's going to the 61st precinct right now."

Polo Man says, "Thanks, son. I will fly in tonight and then you can let me in on this."

At the 61st precinct, Ice says to Officer Anderson, "You guys know this is some dirty shit with one of you broke clowns getting paid from this fake bust!"

Officer Anderson replies, "You better shut your mouth, little punk!"

Ice says, "I got your punk!"

They process Ice and take his picture, but because he's under the age of 18, they only held him for questions.

Officer Anderson asks, "Ice, who are you selling drugs for?"

Ice replies, "I don't know what you're trying to pull off, but my lawyer will answer your questions."

Officer Anderson says, "I don't see a lawyer here right now, and if you want to see another day outside these walls you better come up with some answers, boy!"

Meanwhile, Diamond calls Victoria to tell her what happened. Then, Victoria calls Christian, who then calls Jose. They all meet at Christian's house.

Peter receives a call from James about what happened, so he decides to leave the hospital to drive over to the 61st precinct. As he gets on his bike and drives down the road, he notices a grey BMW following him. He sees that the car is about 4 cars behind him. Peter turns down a dark alley.

The BMW just stops at the corner in front of the alley. Peter gets a good look at the license plate as the grey BMW speeds off – XKG 123. Peter calls James.

He says, "Hey, man, I've just been followed."

James replies, "By who?"

Peter says, "I don't know, but I got the make of the car and the tag number." Peter gives him the information and they hang up.

10 minutes later, James calls Peter back and says, "The car that was following you belongs to a Gerald Wang. Do you know him, Peter?"

Peter replies, "He followed me to my sister's hospital to invite me to a party at the Big Wong this Saturday."

James says, "Something is wrong, man. I have heard this name come up many times during conversations at the house. You must be careful, Peter, if you go to this party."

Peter replies, "Thanks, James, for the advice. But right now I must go to the police station to check on Ice."

Back at the 61$^{st}$ precinct, Harry Weinstein, Polo Man's lawyer, arrives to help Ice. He is one of the biggest lawyers in New York. His clients include P. Diddy, Jay-Z, Russell Simmons, and Jimmy "The Fox" Marchetti.

He says to the officers holding Ice, "Hello, Gentlemen, let's get down to business. First, you have a minor here brought up on drug charges that you know and I know were planted in his home by one of you corrupt cops. So, I would advise you to let this kid go because when I finish with this case some heads are going to fly. Trust me." Mr. Weinstein is successful in getting Ice out of jail.

They exit the police station and get into his black

Rolls Royce Phantom and drive back to Ice's apartment. Meanwhile, en route to the apartment, his father calls Mr. Weinstein, "Hey, Harry."

He replies, "Hey, Polo, what's up?"

Polo says, "Listen, I've got some information about that break in from an anonymous caller who has tapped into the FBI phone system. There was a secret break in at my house and it went wrong. I don't know all the details, but the two people involved were FBI Agent Michael Collier and rookie cop Jeff Hayes."

Mr. Weinstein replies, "Officer Hayes is already on probation because of dirty drug money found in his squad car three months ago. Agent Michael Collier sounds familiar, but I don't quite know from where."

Polo says, "One more thing, the man who gave the instruction was Agent Swartz."

Harry becomes very silent. He says to Polo, "Are you sure?"

Polo replies, "Yes."

Harry says, "This guy's dirty, but smart. We must keep this information to ourselves. I will see you when you get to New York."

Polo asks, "Can I talk to my son?"

Harry puts Ice on the phone.

"Hey son."

Ice says. "Hey dad."

"You alright, son?"

Ice replies, "Yeah, but these cops planted coke in our house."

Polo responds, "I know this, son, and I'm going to find

out the punks that pulled this off. Don't you worry. How is Diamond?"

Ice responds, "She's at the apartment waiting."

Polo says, "Ok, you go home, get your things packed, and go to the studio apartment in Queens. Stay there until I get in town. I love you, son."

Ice says, "I love you, too, dad." Ice gives the phone back to Mr. Weinstein.

"You must be very careful. I don't want anything to happen to you."

Ice replies, "Ok, sir."

Mr. Weinstein then drops him off at Ice's apartment.

Meanwhile, Peter sees that Ice is picked up by someone in a black Rolls Royce car and he heads for the hospital. Back at Ice's apartment, Diamond hears the phone ring and answers it. The caller has a Spanish accent.

"Have you seen my sister, Milda?"

Diamond asks, "Who is this?"

The caller replies, "This is her sister Rita Hernandez. Milda has not come here to pick up her daughter yet."

Diamond says, "Oh my God, did she call you?"

Rita replies, "No, she didn't call. We are all very worried about her, and her daughter Emily is very afraid."

Diamond says, "Can she stay with you until we find her mother?"

Rita says, "Yes, of course. And what should I do?"

Diamond says, "Call the police and tell them everything."

Meanwhile, Officer Jeff Hayes and Agent Michael Collier tell Swartz what happened.

Swartz becomes pissed, "You did what? You stupid shits!

I tell you to plant drugs in the house and you guys didn't check to see if anyone was home?!"

Agent Collier replies, "No, man, this woman came in while we were already there!"

Swartz says, "Didn't you clear the move for that day as to what activity, if any, would be happening that day?"

Agent Collier responds, "Yes, the woman comes each day, but leaves by 2pm."

Swartz barks, "Well, she came back, and now we've got a homicide on our hands with a massive police search and missing person reports! This could really backfire! Plus, I heard Harry Weinstein is the lawyer for Ice and Polo Man!"

# CHAPTER 9

Back in Hong Kong, Lim plans to catch a cargo ship and leave for New York City. He should be in New York by Friday of this week. In Hong Kong, Daniel Wang is investigating the prison escape and other people who knew Lim, but he's losing time. It's been 3 weeks since Lim has escaped, and the only possible sighting since then was the killing at the factory. But that could have been a disgruntled employee.

Lim is spending his last day with Tina, his girl. She equips him with money in American currency, a passport, and his ninja bag. They make love in the grass corn field outside of the farm house.

Back at the hospital, Jenny is meditating in the room and working on some fight routines. Around 10:30pm, she hears a knock on the door. It's her close friend and daughter of Mr. Jackson, Tonya.

Jenny says, "Wait just a minute. Who is it?"

Tonya replies, "It's me, Tonya."

Jenny opens the door, "Oh my, I miss you! Come in!"

Tonya enters and kisses Jenny. Tonya says, "I hear you're doing much better. I am so happy for you."

Jenny says, "Thanks. How is Mr. Jackson?"

Tonya replies, "He's doing much better. He asks about you all the time. How is Peter?"

Jenny says, "He's ok, but I sense some kind of trouble in him. He doesn't know it, but I'm not always asleep when he visits me, and I hear his thoughts. I feel there is some kind of danger, but I don't know what's wrong."

Tonya says, "Do you know a Mr. Swartz?"

Jenny replies, "Yes, the mean security guard, I do know him."

Tonya says, "Well, he's causing some problems, and my dad feels that he is a threat to us."

Jenny responds, "I really like your father, and Peter talks about him all the time. If any harm comes to your dad, I will kill him."

Tonya looks at Jenny, "What did you say?"

Jenny replies, "I'm sorry, but I don't want anything to happen to you or Mr. Jackson."

Back at Ice's apartment, the police return and knock on the door. Ice opens the door, and Detective Jerry Miller and his partner Detective Gregg Wilson are standing there.

Detective Miller identifies himself and asks, "Can we come in?" Ice lets them in, and Miller asks, "When was the last time you saw Milda Hernandez?"

Ice replies, "She comes when I'm in school, but if she needs to finish my cleaning or preparing for the next day, she might stay until at least 6pm. But that's not normal for her."

Detective Miller says, "Let me rephrase this, Mr. Divine, when did you see her last?"

Ice says, "It was yesterday before school at about 8 am."

Miller asks, "Does she call you on your cell phone to tell you if she is not coming or will be late?"

Ice replies, "Very seldom. She's very dependable. She's never missed a day or even misses a day for vacation or when she's sick."

Diamond says, "I found something of hers."

Miller asks, "What is it?"

Diamond says, "Her earring was found in the kitchen on the floor."

Miller asks, "Was there anything else unusual you can tell me?"

Ice says, "The food was in the refrigerator and it was not cooked. She always prepares our dinner and leaves it in the microwave."

Officer Miller tells Officer Wilson to investigate the kitchen. Ice, Officer Miller, and Diamond go to the family room and sit down.

Miller asks, "When did you call Mrs. Hernandez's sister Rita?"

Diamond replies, "We didn't, she called us."

Officer Miller asks, "Do you know if she had a boyfriend or anyone close to her other than her sister and daughter?"

Ice replies, "I only hear about her sister Rita and her daughter Emily."

Officer Wilson comes into the family room after investigating the kitchen. He says, "I can smell a small amount of bleach on your kitchen floor and some on your wall beside the entrance of the kitchen. I will need a forensics team to analyze this further. Most of the time this much bleach is used to clean up something."

The detectives proceed to survey the entire area inside and outside the apartment. They determine that there was, in fact, blood in the kitchen and on the wall. They also see bullet fragments in the blood on the wall. The entire apartment was converted into a homicide crime scene area. Detectives Miller and Wilson discuss the possibilities of a shooting at the apartment around 2pm.

Officer Miller tells Ice and Diamond, "Gather all your things. I'm sorry, you're going to have to leave this apartment. Is there someplace you can go?"

Ice replies, "I'm ok."

Detective Miller gives Ice his card and says, "If you can think of anything or anyone that would want to hurt Mrs. Hernandez, call me."

Ice phones his dad, "Dad, guess what? The police found blood in the kitchen and possible bullet fragments in some blood on the wall. They think that Mrs. Hernandez was shot in our apartment."

Polo says, "Who have you told this to?"

Ice replies, "No one, Dad."

Polo says, "Don't say anything to anyone! Go to the studio in Queens. I will call Mr. Weinstein. Stay put."

Ice replies, "Ok, Dad."

Polo says, "Be careful, son."

Ice promises, "I will, Dad."

Meanwhile, during the investigation, the forensic team found blood on the sidewalk outside the apartment building.

Detective Lopez says, "I also found what appears to be a

parking ticket on the street in close proximity to the blood. Whoever was parked here could be a suspect. We must call the parking authority to get the tag number and the time of every ticket given in this vicinity yesterday between the hours of 1 pm and 4 pm."

Back in Hong Kong, Lim boards the Hong Kong International cargo ship. He gets aboard the ship through a side door and enters the ship's lowest deck. This area has boxes tagged for New York Harbor. Lim feels safe here. He soon finds out that the ship is not just for cargo, but illegal drugs and Chinese immigrants fleeing the country to live in the United States. As Lim pulls out his blankets to go to sleep, he realizes that he's not alone. He looks under a crate and sees a young boy staring at him.

Lim says, "Hello, are you here by yourself?"

The kid replies, "I'm here with my mom."

Lim asks, "Where is your mom?"

The kid replies, "Looking for food."

Lim asks, "What is your name?"

The kid says, "Michael Chin."

Lim asks further, "Why are you on this boat?"

The kid replies, "My mom says our life could be better like my uncle Chin who sells fish in New York."

Lim says, "Do you want to share some beans and fruit?"

"Yes," says Michael.

His mother then returns. She is alarmed by Lim's presence. She asks with a frightened look, "Who are you?"

Her son Michael says, "He's a very nice man and he has some food, Mom. Sit down and eat, it's ok."

So they sit together and eat.

While eating, Lim says, "Quiet," and holds up a finger to his mouth.

Someone is coming. It's a cargo security guard walking down the stairs scanning the room with a flashlight. The little kid Michael forgot to put his feet up while sitting under the crate. The security guard shines the light on the crate and sees the little feet hanging down. Lim realizes that if the security guard captures Michael that more security personnel will come down to the cargo hold, and they may even kill the kid and his mother. As the security guard gets closer, Lim sneaks up behind the cop with his rope and chokes the security guard to death. Lim then stuffs the cop's body under some bags of coal. The mother and son are terrified watching this. The mother prepares to run up the stairs with her son.

Lim stops her and reassures her, "Don't be afraid, I won't hurt you. That cop would have killed you and your son for sure."

She reluctantly comes back to their secret hiding spot.

In the meantime, Daniel, Mr. Wang's son, is still looking for Lim in Hong Kong. He might have a small lead. Someone from the prison that knew Lim told a Chinese police detective that if you give him a lesser sentence he would provide the name and location of Lim's beloved girlfriend Tina. This prisoner, Mia Tang, was in the same cell early in Lim's sentence. Detective Foo Si Wi gives Daniel the needed information. He intends to find Tina and question her. Daniel drives to Tina's country town. Daniel is a very skilled fighter and very good with weapons. He finds the house that the inmate described. He knocks on the door, but

Tina's not inside. She's in the field out back picking corn. Daniel breaks into her small house and waits for her. She finishes picking the corn and approaches her house. Because of her deep involvement with Lim, Tina is wise and street smart. She never comes to her home without checking for footprints at her front door. This time she notices one set of footprints by the door, so she enters the house through the back door. She opens the door. Daniel hears the door open in the back of the house.

Tina says, "I know you're in my house. If you're not family, you're illegally trespassing in my home, and I would strongly advise you to leave NOW!"

Daniel responds, "You don't have any rights when you help fugitives!"

Tina replies, "I don't know what you're talking about!"

He says, "Yes, I think you do. I have proof, so don't play with me, you little bitch! If you don't help me, you're going to take his place!"

Daniel runs toward Tina. Tina jumps up, pulls out her samurai sword, and slices Daniel's arm. Daniel pulls out his gun and fires a shot at her, but he misses. Tina sprints out the front door and leaps up onto the roof with catlike agility.

Daniel comes out the front door after her and says, "I will kill you!" As his arm bleeds profusely from the deep gash Tina inflicted on him.

Tina jumps off the roof onto Daniel's back and slices the blade of her sword down Daniel's shoulder, he crumbles to the ground. She turns him over to kill him, but stops and says, "I won't kill you, but you listen to me, Lim has done you no harm, and you put him in jail for no reason. You can put me in jail or even kill me. Lim will never be stopped, and if I were you I would tell every person who betrayed him to run for their lives because death is sure to find them!" Tina stands up and leaves him to bleed to death on her front steps.

The Hong Kong police now arrive at Tina's home and they find Daniel's dead body on her front steps.

Officer Lou Chi, the supervisor of the cops, says to the other officers, "I want a full investigation of the crime scene. I want to know who this man is and why he would be at this house with a gun in his hand. Also, we need to find the owner of the farmhouse."

After reviewing all the information at the scene, they find out that the murder victim is the co-owner of a New York City restaurant, one Daniel Wang. The Hong Kong Police contact the New York City Police Department and report the death. Back at the Big Wong restaurant, Mr. Wang gets a phone call. It's Detective Henry Brooks of the New York City Police Crime Lab.

"Hello, is this Mr. Wang?"

Wang replies, "Yes."

Brooks says, "Do you have a son named Daniel Wang?"

Wang immediately knew something was wrong, "Yes."

Brooks says, "I'm sorry to tell you this, but your son was found dead in Hong Kong. He was murdered."

Out of his hurt and pain, Wang asks, "Who killed him?"

Brooks replies, "We don't have that information right now, but I will give it to you when we have a suspect."

Wang says, "Do you know how he was killed?"

Brooks replies, "It appears to be from a knife or some kind of sword."

Wang never in a million years ever thought that something like this would happen to his only son. Wang says, "I want the lead detective's name who's handling the investigation in Hong Kong."

Brooks replies, "It's Lou Chin."

Wang says, "Thank you," and hangs up the phone.

Mr. Wang's brother, Bruce Wang, calls Mr. Wang. "I'm very sorry about Daniel. He didn't contact me while he was here in Hong Kong for protection. If we want the person or persons who did this, we must act fast in order to slow down the Hong Kong Police Department with questioning the family and discovering our ties with Lim, the fugitive."

Mr. Wang replies, "Yes, we must be very careful. This investigation could expose us, and they could discover what Daniel was really doing in Hong Kong."

In the meantime, the NYPD get a break in the death of Milda Hernandez. They found out that the car that was parked outside the house at 2 pm was a police vehicle driven by Officer Jeff Hayes. Jeff's a dirty cop. He's been on suspension for dirty drug money that was found in his squad car three months ago. If this information is true, he could be charged with murder. The police also found blood stains in the trunk of his car, a shoe, and another earring that matches the one that was found in Polo's kitchen. All this connects Hayes to the crime, but as of right now, police detectives are withholding information until they get the reason Mr. Hayes was at the crime scene and if there were any accomplices involved that could have been cops or related to police involvement as well because the home was supposed to have drugs in it from a search warrant. This is a big mystery for the NYPD, but they do know that the parking ticket doesn't lie and his car was parked outside the building at that time with the meter expired on that date and time.

It's the end of the month, and Swartz and his wife are about to fly to Colorado for two weeks. The hotel and resort will be having its annual art exhibit with the feature artist being Susan Swartz.

It's Saturday. The big party at the Big Wong is tonight, and a guest has just arrived in New York City by cargo boat. Lim just exited the boat wearing his police uniform, and he hails down a taxi to go visit the New York City police station.

He arrives at the station, walks up to the police officer sitting at the front desk and says, "Hello, my name is Woo Chi Pong, and I'm here to help you find your killer."

The police officer calls Detective Sanders. He greets Lim and invites him back to his desk where they sit.

Sanders asks, "Would you like some tea or coffee?"

Lim replies, "Tea would be fine." Lim says, "We've had several killings in Hong Kong that are similar to the reports that I've been seeing in the news about your killings here in New York. I feel this could be part of the same crime family that has caused our city so many problems. I feel they may have moved to New York."

Sanders replies, "Let's keep you undercover. Only report to me. Is there anything you will need in New York?"

Lim replies, "No, just a place to stay."

Sanders says, "That shouldn't be a problem. Here's my

card and personal contact cell phone number. Call me if you need anything, Mr. Pong."

Lim replies, "Thank you." Lim exits the police station and takes a cab to Canal Street in Chinatown. He enters a Chinese café called Mr. Liu's Place. As he is sitting, he orders some rice and noodles. Beside him he overhears two gentleman talking in a Chinese dialect about the big party for Mr. Wang tonight. The men discuss how all the big shots of New York and the Hong Kong-based business associates will be there. Lim decides to find a way to be invited to the big party. He walks over to the two gentlemen's table and in Chinese says, "Hello, I just arrived in New York. My name is Pong, and I couldn't help but overhearing your conversation about the restaurant called The Big Wong. I heard about it in China. Is it as nice as what I've heard about it, and can you tell me how to get there?"

The older Chinese man says, "It's in Chinatown on the corner of Canal and Nicholas Street."

Lim replies, "Thank you." He walks back over to his table and finishes his noodles.

Swartz gets a phone call from Mr. Marchetti. "Swartz, you've got a lot of problems. I heard about the drug search that went bad. You seem to be slipping. You got my money yet!?"

Swartz replies, "No, sir, I'm still waiting on that, sir."

Marchetti says, "At the rate you're going, you might not have a job. I don't want to read about you in the obituaries or the front page of the New York Times saying *FBI Agent Gets Caught in Sting Operation* before I get my money, you stupid fool!"

Swartz replies, "I won't, Mr. Marchetti, I'm going out of town. I will get it to you next week."

Marchetti replies, "Okay, Swartz, you've got until Friday or say goodbye to your lovely wife Susan."

Swartz says, "No problem, I will get the money."

In the meantime, Jenny's health has improved so much that the doctors have allowed her mother to take her home. Her brother has been waiting for this day for a very long time. She enters the apartment and Peter greets her with a big kiss and says, "Hi, Jenny! How are you feeling?" Jenny responds, "Good. I can't wait to go out to a party! I've missed so much time with no fun in the hospital!" Peter replies, "Guess what? There's a surprise party tonight at the Big Wong restaurant. Would you like to come?" Jenny quickly responds, "Yes! I would love to!" Peter's mom asks, "Are you guys hungry?" They both state, "Yes!" Mrs. Wong begins to cook. Peter assures his mom, "Is it okay for me to take Jenny to the party tonight?" Mrs. Wong replies, "Yes, it would be good for her but don't stay too late." Peter says, "I know."

Now it's Saturday evening and despite the bad news from Hong Kong, Mr. Wang still has his party. The best rock band from New York is hired to play music. The restaurant is decorated with very nice flowers. It's about 8 pm and the guests begin to arrive. Jenny and Peter arrive at the party and have to stand at the door to wait because of the long lines of guests. Finally, Gerald Wang sees Peter and Jenny in front of the restaurant. Gerald says, "Peter, follow me! I will get you in with me. After all, it's my birthday!" Peter replies, "Okay, thanks!" Gerald asks, "Is this Jenny?" Peter says, "Yes." Gerald comments, "She looks good! She must be

very happy." Jenny says, "I'm great!" They enter the restaurant through a side door. Also standing in line is Swartz. He
stops by to give his respect to Mr. Wang before he leaves for
Colorado. Across the street, Lim is standing and watching
the guests pour into the restaurant. Swartz spots Lim across
the street and says to himself, "That's strange, I've never
seen a Chinese cop in Chinatown. I must meet this cop."
Meanwhile, inside, Mr. Wang starts his celebration in the
VIP section with Mr. Marchetti and Swartz. Downstairs
are Peter and Jenny. Finally, Lim comes up to the doorman.
He says, "Hey, man, I'm here. I was sent by the NYPD to
keep the crowd control level down." "Okay," says the doorman and he lets Lim enter the restaurant. Lim sits at the
bar downstairs. Finally, Gerald enters the room and thanks
everyone for coming. He says, "Please enjoy yourself, it's my
30th birthday and I plan to party!" The guests begin clapping
wildly for him and yelps and screams erupt from the crowd.

In the meantime, Jenny has to visit the ladies room.
She overhears two gentlemen talking in the hallway beside
the women's bathroom. One man says, "So, Swartz, do you
think that Chinese kid at the private school, Peter, could
have anything to do with Mr. Jackson's off-duty cop killings?" Swartz replies, "I don't know." The first man says,
"Did you know that Mr. Jackson's daughter is real close
friends with Peter's sister, Jenny?" Swartz replies, "Yes, I
know this, but she's sick in the hospital." The first says,
"Not true. I heard she was released on Friday. I found a
kid from that school who says he has heard rumors that
Peter is a karate expert and he teaches a self-defense class
in Manhattan at night." Swartz replies, "I'm going to get

someone to tail him for a while after this party is over." The first man says, "Okay." Swartz and the men rejoin the party. In the club suite, Jenny hears all this but doesn't quite know why this man Swartz would want to harm her or Peter but she is prepared to kill him if necessary. Swartz tells the girl he is with to excuse him so he can visit the men's room. At the same time, Peter tells Jenny that he needs to run to the men's room. Swartz gets to the bathroom first. While Swartz is washing his hands, Peter enters. Swartz sees Peter before Peter sees him.

Swartz calls his boy who he was speaking with previously beside the ladies room to meet him in the men's room, "I got that little punk Chinese shit Peter in the men's room. Come Quick! I want to question him right now." At that time, Peter is in the stall and overhears Swartz's cell phone conversation. He also realizes this is a set up. All of a sudden, the door to the men's room opens. It's Lim. He enters the bathroom.

Peter looks under the stall and sees the pants and shoes of a policeman but he doesn't recognize who or what kind of police officer wears that type of uniform. He realizes that it's a Chinese cop. But they don't have Chinese cops in Chinatown. Peter stays in the stall. Swartz's friend enters the bathroom. He says, "Hey, Swartz, what's up?" Swartz replies, "Behind the third stall to the left is some shit I need cleaned!" The friends says, "Okay, boss, no problem." Lim sees that someone's in the third stall so he acts like he's washing his hands and waits. When Swartz's friend pushes the door of the stall open, Peter kicks him in the balls. The thug goes down. Swartz screams, "Hey! What's going on?"

and pulls out his gun. Lim swiftly kicks the gun out of
Swartz's hand, throws Swartz into the wall and elbows him
in the head. Swartz crumbles to the ground. Swartz's thug
tries to pull out his gun and Lim kicks the gun out of the
thug's hand as well. He throws the thug into the wall and
fiercely kicks the man in his thigh, breaking it! The thug
crumbles to the ground grunting in pain. Lim hits the thug
in the head with a blow that knocks him completely out.
Lim then takes the man's handcuffs and cuffs both guys to
the bathroom stall door. Hearing all the commotion, Peter
storms out of the stall and attempts to kick Lim, however,
Lim blocks the kick and says, "Who are you?" Peter replies,
"You want to know this before you kill me?" Lim says, "No,
you look like my brother, Peter." Peter stops in his tracks
and put his hands to his face and asks, "Who are you?"
Lim replies, "I am Lim." Peter replies, "You can't be Lim.
He's been dead for fifteen years!" Lim says, "No, Peter, I
was in a Hong Kong prison. They didn't notify any family
members with the truth and they hid me there all this time.
I escaped earlier this month and came to New York to find
the people who betrayed our family. Let's get out of here.
Where's Jenny?" The stunned Peter replies, "She's here at the
party." Lim says, "We must leave quickly because the men
who tried to hurt you are also associates of the men who
betrayed us." Peter finds Jenny in the crowd and says, "We
must leave. There is a bad situation here for us." Peter and
Jenny meet Lim out in front of the restaurant. Lim says to
Peter and Jenny, "Don't tell your mother or anyone else that
I am alive. We must keep it a secret until I find the people

responsible for my death. I will keep in touch with you by old ninja code. Do you remember, Peter?"

Peter replies, "Yes." Jenny says, "I love you, Lim." Lim begins to cry and says, "I must leave now." Back inside the party, one of Gerald's bodyguards finds Swartz and his thug in the bathroom beat down, bleeding and handcuffed to the stall door. Gerald calls Mr. Wang and they all meet in his private office. Swartz and the thug are brought into the office. Swartz says, "I need to go to a hospital. My head is spinning. The thug, whose name is Tom Kipper, says, "Yeah, I think my leg is broken. Please help me." Mr. Wang barks at them, "I must know who did this to you!" Swartz says, "I think it was a Chinese policeman but I'm not sure. It happened so fast!" The thug says, "It was that little Chinese boy, Peter. He kicked me." Swartz looks at him and says, "But he never left the stall." The thug asks, "Then who broke my leg?" Swartz replies, "I don't know who he is but he is not a policeman." Wang says, "I want the boy Peter at my office by tomorrow, no one crashes Gerald's honorable birthday party! This is a disrespect to me and my family! Swartz, you better be truthful to me or your family will never leave New York alive. So go and don't come back here again! You've brought trouble to our family and we have a phantom assassin because of this! Swartz and the thug are transported to the New York General Hospital by ambulance which happens to be the same hospital that Mr. Jackson was transferred to after the second attempt on his life. The doctors and nurses put Swartz in a private room where they run tests on his head injury and they confirm that he has suffered a concussion. The thug has a broken right fibula thigh bone which will require surgery to repair the injury. Swartz stays overnight to check on his friend.

Meanwhile, Jenny takes a cab to the hospital to check on Mr. Jackson. He is still in bad shape and might need six more weeks to recover fully. Jenny enters Mr. Jackson's room and reads to him. Mr. Jackson falls asleep. Swartz is up walking around the hospital halls trying to find Mr. Jackson's room. He finds a nurse on the critical ward floor and says, "I'm from the FBI and I was injured in a shootout. The people who I'm dealing with are coming here soon for Mr. Jackson. We need to move him to another room. I know that the NYPD told you this earlier but there are possible suspects who are trying to kill him. Please help me. He is my best friend." At this time, Jenny goes to the snack room to get a soda and some chips. In the meantime, the nurse takes Swartz to Mr. Jackson's room to move him. Swartz and the nurse enter the room. She says, "Mr. Jackson, we must move you. You're in danger." Mr. Jackson opens his eyes and sees Swartz standing before him. He can't talk because of the tubes in his mouth but he signals the nurse with hand signals, "NO." She doesn't understand though. Jenny enters the room, sees Swartz and loudly screams, "Call the police!!" This man is a killer!" The nurse replies, "Calm down! Swartz is here to help Mr. Jackson." At that moment, Swartz pulls out his gun to shoot Jenny. He fires but misses her. The terrified nurse screams, "What are you doing?" and Swartz shoots her at point blank range killing her instantly. Jenny leaps behind him and kicks the gun from his hand. He tries to grab her. She punches him in his throat. He drops to his knees. Jenny grabs a pair of scissors from the dressing table and stabs Swartz in the temple of his head and then darts around behind him and breaks his neck. Swartz is dead. She says to Mr. Jackson, "I am sorry. I must leave." At that time, she exits. The doctors and police guards find Mr. Jackson in his room unharmed but quite shaken.

Jenny leaves the hospital and finds her way back home. She tells her mother what happened and falls into a deep sleep. The next morning she becomes deathly ill once again. Peter comes home and immediately calls the doctor who comes over. After checking her vital signs, the doctor says, "Oh no. We need to get her back to the hospital immediately! Something's terribly wrong!" She's taken by ambulance back to the hospital and placed in the critical condition unit. Upon running more tests, the doctors conclude that the cancer has returned. The head doctor somberly explains to her, "Chemotherapy and radiation are futile at this point. The cancer has spread to all of her major organs. She's not going to make it. I'm so very sorry." Upon hearing the news, Mrs. Wong collapses on the floor of the hospital waiting room sobbing and shaking. As Peter tries to comfort her, he feels a wave of shock and grief crash over him like a tsunami. The next two weeks are painstaking for Peter and Mrs. Wong as they watch Jenny deteriorate day by day. They sleep at the hospital around the clock. The boys visit on a regular basis and try to be strong for Peter and his mother but the mood in Jenny's room is heart wrenching. At this point, she is being kept alive by the machines. It's 11pm, Peter is sitting next to her bed and Mrs. Wong is sleeping in the chair next to Jenny's bed. He stares at her as she sleeps. Her eyes open, she turns her head and looks at

Peter. "Peter," she whispers. Peter whispers, "Yes, Jenny, I'm here." He grabs her hand. Jenny whispers, "All the violence, all the pain in this world, do you think there's somewhere better?" A tear streams down Peter's face. "Yes, Jenny, there is no doubt." A tear streams down the side of Jenny's face. "Do you think I'll go there?" Peter replies, "Yes. Absolutely." Jenny says, "Peter, I love you." Peter replies, "Jenny, I love you too." Suddenly, the EKG monitor tracking her heartbeat speeds up. She struggles to breath. Mrs. Wong wakes up from the sounds of the EKG monitor which is now bleeping rapidly and screams, "Oh, my God, Oh no!" Mrs. Wong grabs Jenny's other hand. The EKG monitor is at a fever pitch right now, Jenny stops breathing and the sound of the EKG monitor flat lines to a steady sound. Jenny's eyes slowly close. She dies.

Jenny's funeral is held at Saint Mary's Cemetery in New York City. After the service at the church, the members of the funeral procession drive to the cemetery through the streets of New York City. Peter and Mrs. Wong ride in the family vehicle following the vehicle with the casket. Jose is driving his SL500 Silver Mercedes, James is driving his Range Rover Truck, Ice and Diamond are driving in the Cayenne Porsche and Christian and Victoria are driving in Mr. Snow's BMW. Multiple other vehicles follow behind them including Mr. Jackson and Tonya. At the cemetery, Jenny's friends and loved ones gather around the grave site and listen to the priest's solemn benediction. Peter holds his sobbing mother while Mr. Jackson holds his sobbing daughter. As tough as the boys are, they cannot hold back their tears. Everyone's devastated. There are other guests at Jenny's funeral though; uninvited guests. They are watching from afar through binoculars. They wear badges and coats that have FBI on the back. They are still suspicious and are trying to figure out how a group of teenagers were able to fool Mr. Marchetti and Mr. Wang's plans. While the corrupt FBI conduct their surveillance on the funeral, someone's conducting surveillance on them. It's Lim. This is only the beginning, Lim thinks to himself. It's only the beginning.

# ABOUT THE AUTHOR

Born in Baltimore, MD, raised by a military step-father who was enlisted in the Air Force is where young Leon King learned about different cultures in life. It was through his traveling in Europe that he learned to appreciate art.

Leon has always been a dreamer, very enthusiastic and a person who enjoys the finer things in life. This characteristic in life compelled him to be successful in everything that he desired. He is a devoted family man and a very faithful man of God. This attitude keeps him burning and always looking for new ideas and new inventions to explore. When his young son told him that he was tired of reading the books at the local bookstore, fire burned inside of him and he vowed to write a book that son would read.

His love for food, fashion, and writing has allowed him to inspire others everywhere. He believes that his gifts will make room for him at the table of great men.

Printed in the United States
By Bookmasters